# THE DEVIL YOU KNOW

# THE DEVIL YOU KNOW

*Nick Englebrecht #1*

## K.H. KOEHLER

The Monster Factory

# THE DEVIL YOU KNOW

A NICK ENGLEBRECHT MYSTERY

K.H. KOEHLER

The Devil You Know (The Nick Englebrecht Mysteries Book 1)
Copyright © 2012 K.H. Koehler

All rights reserved

The characters and events portrayed in this book are fictitious. Any similarity to real persons, living or dead is coincidental and not intended by the author.

No part of this book may be reproduced, or stored in a retrieval system, or transmitted in any form or by any means, electronic, mechanical, photocopying, recording, or otherwise, without express written permission of the publisher.

Paperback ISBN: 979-8-8692-1732-5

Ebook ISBN: 979-8-8692-1733-2

No part of this book was created using Artificial Intelligence.

Cover design by: KH Koehler Design
https://khkoehler.net
Printed in the United States of America

# CONTENTS

| | |
|---|---|
| 1 | 1 |
| 2 | 12 |
| 3 | 21 |
| 4 | 29 |
| 5 | 38 |
| 6 | 45 |
| 7 | 59 |
| 8 | 69 |
| 9 | 78 |

| 10 | 90 |
| 11 | 102 |
| 12 | 109 |
| 13 | 122 |
| 14 | 130 |
| 15 | 145 |
| 16 | 151 |
| 17 | 161 |
| 18 | 169 |
| 19 | 182 |
| 20 | 193 |
| *About The Author* | 202 |

# | 1 |

LIKE A BAD detective novel, it started with a woman.

Not just *a* woman. *The* woman.

In the Dashiell Hammett books, it's always some curvalicious widow in black trailing behind her own particular brand of crawling chaos. I got the exact same feeling from the redhead, though she wasn't wearing the traditional black dress and veil when she barged into the shop, the door clomping shut behind her. Rather, she was dressed in the watery blue uniform of Molly's Steakhouse six blocks down on what's locally known here in Blackwater as the Strip. They serve overpriced porterhouse steaks and underpriced beer, which is its main attraction. You can drink yourself silly, and the bill won't hurt as bad.

I didn't know her, but the redhead lurched to a stop in front of the display counter, looked me straight in the eyes, and said, "There's a man following me."

I immediately knew a few things about her: 1. she was out too late; 2. she wasn't local because locals have more sense than to walk alone on the Strip at 11:15 at night; and 3. she was curvalicious. Number 3 is irrelevant to this story, but I figured I'd mention it anyway.

Emergencies have a way of solidifying a relationship between strangers. I felt responsible for her. The red hair and curves didn't hurt at all.

"Is he coming?" I asked.

"Yes," she answered. She was breathless and disheveled from what was likely a brisk, terror-filled, six-block jog.

"Did he see you come in here?"

"Maybe. I don't know!"

Before she could say another word, I slipped around the counter, snagged her by the wrist, then dragged her down into the kneehole beneath the counter where my partner Morgana and I keep the late-night shop essentials—keys, flashlight, special orders, the lock box, bottles of Aquafina, and a dented aluminum baseball bat.

Don't ask about the bat. That's a rather grim and uneventful story for another day.

The redhead fit as if she was made for the kneehole. She started to protest, but I sat on the stool behind the counter, resumed piecing together the set of Egyptian bezel that Morgana had been ragging me about all day, and said in a casual whisper, "Here he comes."

Within seconds, the hulking shadow of a man slowed outside the shop.

Curiosities, the shop Morgana and I run, is located in an old brownstone at the northern tip of the Strip. It's one of the older buildings, built around the time of the Depression when Blackwater was transitioning from a silver mining town to a tourist trap for broke upper-class New Yorkers. As a result, the shop, like many of them here, is barely large enough to change your mind in. It's made smaller still by the shelves of trinkets and souvenirs we sold to the surviving descendants of those same upper-class New Yorkers—crystals, medicinals, books, tarot cards kits, carefully color-coded candles, incense burners, how-to DVDs, and racks of imported jewelry. In the hotter months, the shop becomes a head-spinning miasma of floral and sandalwood incense. There's no big picture window like the antique shop next door, and no shiny new glass fronting like Dollar General across the street. If anything, Curiosities looks like a subdued Irish pub with a faded green awning and an old-fashioned hanging plaque above the door, the only things to denote it as a public establishment. Our return clients buy from the back room, mostly elixirs for money, sex, and happiness; the rest is tourist fodder. The door is made of actual church glass from a local cathedral torn down in 1963, and virtually every stick of wood inside the shop hailed from a church auction.

I recognized the shadow before it entered my shop, but I didn't believe it was actually Malach until I saw him stomp in. Malach and I have a history. He works for a private agency and does wetwork. He'd love to shoot my ass but he has no jurisdiction, nor any evidence of wrongdoing. He's big and Aryan blond, and he has that whole ex-Navy SEAL thing going on, if you're into that kind of thing. He dresses in more oiled patent leather than a gay Otaku biker coming off a summer-long anime kick, but he manages to pull it off somehow. I have to admire that about the guy.

He creak-walked up to me and put a very large, very gold handgun in my face. There was script on the barrel in a language no human being on Earth can read.

"Where is she?" he grumbled, his voice coming from deep within his leather-clad chest. The floorboards faintly vibrated.

Malach is taller than I am and twice as wide. He could break me over his knee if I gave him just cause. But I know how to play the game. The thing about Malach is, he talks tough and gets his way. He's a bully, and bullies are boring. They're predictable.

I studied the miniature cannon in his big, leather-gloved hand. A .60 caliber round was lodged up there somewhere, ammunition that could make a donut of a man's head.

"Lose your girlfriend, Malach?" I asked, going back to the display.

"Don't fuck with me, Nick. I'm really not into you tonight."

"We breaking up?"

Malach smirked. Malach never smiles, only smirks. I think it's in the Tough Guy Manual somewhere. "One good reason, Nick. What I wouldn't do to dust your ass."

"I dig the slang. But you need to lay off the gangster movies." I smirked. "Just FYI."

"The girl, Nick. Now," Malach said in his own guttural language, which sounds a bit like a muffler dragging across asphalt.

That's another thing about Malach. He has an intense dislike of compound sentences. And English. It's almost a phobia, really. "She ran in and ran out," I said as I alternated scarabs and ankhs in the display boxes. "Ran in the front door and out the back door."

"Where's your back door?"

"Never on the first date. You know that."

Malach lowered his gun and thought about what I'd said. Double entendres are not his strong suit. I blame his education. Sighing, I decided to let him off the hook. Looking up into his dead frosty blue eyes, I said, "In the back?"

Malach stomped around the counter and passed through the beaded curtain behind me. Since the girl was in the kneehole under the counter, my body blocked her from view. I doubt Malach noticed anything. I reflected on the fact that her face was practically pressed against my groin and tried to decide if that was a portent or a happenstance. Malach, meanwhile, was breaking a great deal of glass items in the storeroom. Morgana was going to be livid tomorrow.

Finding nothing, he made his way back out. He could easily have left after that, but I knew he couldn't pass up an opportunity to threaten me on the way out.

Predictable, like I said.

He glared at me as he stomped to the door.

"I'll be back," I said in my best Ahnie impersonation.

"One of these days, Nick..."

"To the moon. Yeah, I know."

* * *

I took the girl upstairs to the loft. That's what I like calling it, anyway. It sounds better than "cold-water flat that hasn't seen an upgrade since the Nixon administration." Actually, it's not as bad as all that, it just isn't much better, and full of old lady things because Morgana's Aunt Lydia lived here until her death seven years ago. I've had worse, much, much worse. I filled the dented teakettle and put it on to heat while I went about the simple tasks of filling two mugs with peppermint tea bags.

Two years ago, we had some bad rains here in northeast Pennsylvania and part of the roof over the kitchen collapsed. Morgana and I wound up replacing the floor and part of the ceiling, but I'd kept the teakettle as a reminder to check the gutters twice a year. I do try to learn from my mistakes.

The girl said her name was Vivian Summers and she worked nights at Molly's Steakhouse, which I already knew. She also said she had just moved to Blackwater. I knew that too. She'd just moved five towns over from White Haven. Moving from White Haven to Blackwater is a little like moving from Upper Manhattan to Bensonhurst. You didn't do it unless you had no other choice.

"You're attending Lincoln Technical?" I asked, leaning my rump against the stove and crossing my arms as I waited on the kettle.

Vivian sat at Aunt Lydia's kitchen table and looked small and nervous. She was very pretty in that old-fashioned way, like a red-haired Marilyn Monroe, minus the mole, not too thin, which doesn't appeal to most guys anyway, despite what Hollywood and *Maxim* magazine would have the world believe.

"Lincoln Culinary, actually. I'm training to be a pastry chef. But that's a great guess."

It wasn't much of a guess. Every young person under the age of twenty-five who moves to Blackwater is either attending the Lincoln group of schools in Allentown or Empire Beauty School in Lehighton. She looked like a serious study horse, so it probably wasn't the beauty school.

I shrugged. "You shouldn't be working so late. The Strip attracts a lot of bad elements after dark."

I probably sounded like her father. Then again, I was her senior by more than twenty years, though she probably didn't realize it. That made me old enough to be the creepy uncle.

Vivian smiled. Her red hair was dark, almost mahogany-black, and her skin clear and white. She had freckles along the bridge of her nose and over the top of her breasts where they peeked out of the open throat of her uniform. I was willing to wager she attracted a lot of attention at Molly's—this little escapade with Malach might even be commonplace for her. She looked young until I saw her eyes. Then I realized she'd been there. It's the same with me.

"You make this place sound like New York," she said a little nervously.

"It is after dark. We get a lot of New Yorkers up here on the weekends."

She shrugged. "I work what hours I can," she answered, sounding defensive now. "I'm paying my own way, you know."

"Then you should get someone to walk you home. A friend or a boyfriend. If you walk these streets alone at night, you're inviting trouble." I hadn't *really* just said that, had I?

"You have a lot to say on the matter."

"I used to be a cop."

She looked surprised by that. Her shoulders relaxed. "For real?"

The kettle started singing so I filled our mugs to the rim with boiling water, transporting one of the mugs over to the table. I set it down in front of Vivian.

"If you're a cop, why don't you drink coffee?" she asked. It was a flirty thing to say, but she didn't make it sound that way. She wrapped her fingers around the mug. I could tell she was still shaken from her run-in with Malach, as any normal human being would be. "Shouldn't you have donuts or something?"

She was a prickly one, Vivian was, and I was pretty sure she was checking me out. Not that I minded. I like to window-shop too.

"I used to be a cop. I'm not anymore," I explained. "Now I just run an occult shop." I stirred my tea with a spoon. "I could get you some donuts if you're hungry, though." The idea of sharing donuts with Vivian was rather appealing even though I detest the very scent of them. My beat partner Peter loved them, and he's been dead going on six years.

She smiled again, a little. "Only if you make coffee."

"I have to drink exotic teas," I said, lifting the steaming mug to my mouth. "It comes with the image, you know?"

"So you're like a wizard."

"Harry Potter is a wizard. I'm a witch."

She thought about that a moment. "I thought witches were women."

"Some are men."

"So you're a cop *and* a witch."

"I *was* a cop. I'm still a witch."

I watched her absorb that.

"Do you cast spells?" she asked.

The steam from the mug made her otherwise redhead-pale face flush. Her Caribbean-blue eyes were sleek and wise in her small, catlike face. I felt something inside me lurch around uncomfortably, something I hadn't felt in a very long time.

"I heard about this place from some girls I know. So do you sell potions and stuff?"

"My partner does that," I said, clutching my mug. I rolled my shoulder where some tension was settling in. "I do séances and channeling, mostly." One thing was certain, Vivian put out some very unusual energies. Very *sexual* energies, and I'm not just being a guy here. The more I talked to her, the stronger I felt. The more focused. I wondered who she was, *what* she was. I wondered if she even knew what she was doing to me. I wondered if she wasn't a supernatural version of an idiot savant. I've met a few in my day. Folks who could move things with their mind when they became upset, that type of thing. It made me wonder even more about her. "Are you interested in magic, Vivian?"

She'd been staring at me so intently that it took her a moment to rouse herself. "Is that some kind of pickup line?" she asked cheekily, setting her mug down.

I decided I liked her fearless expression, the way she didn't back down from me. Most folks do. I'm tall and rangy, which makes me look taller still. I run the only occult shop in town. I talk with a broad Brooklyn accent when I get upset. That's usually enough to scare the bejesus out of any of the locals. I bit back a smile. "I was just wondering about your big blond stalker friend. Seems odd he would follow you."

"You knew him."

"He's...local." Which was a lie, mostly. "Has he followed you in the past?"

"No. I never saw him before in my life." She looked up. She looked on the verge of shivering. She would undoubtedly have nightmares about a big blond leather guy for years to come. Leave it to Malach to always leave a great first impression. "You called him Malach. Is that his name? Who is he?"

"He's...Malach."

"What language was he speaking? I didn't recognize it at all."

I thought about all the complicated lies I could weave together, but the truth was, I could tell she was a smart girl. She'd see through the bullshit. Then I'd have to come clean anyway. Best to cut to the chase. That's what they say in all the detective novels, right? I took a deep breath. "Malach's an angel," I said. "A Seraph, actually. They work under the Archangel Gabriel, who commands the Justice Division. Malach is like a secret agent. He does dirty work for the Throne and has what they call Dominion over Earth, which means he may kill those creatures he deems are a threat to Heaven with impunity, so long as they're not human. In a way, he's like God's hit man."

She looked at me steadily. It took her a long moment to speak. "Malach is God's hit man."

"That's correct."

"And you know this, how? Because you're a witch?"

"Because I'm a daemon. My mother was human but my father was a demon, a fallen angel. Malach is a tracker and has a predilection for daemons. He and his kind believe that all daemons should be erased from existence, that we stand as an affront to God. He may have been tracking you because he believes that you too are a daemon. Do you know much about your parents?"

So there it was. The truth. Or, as I like to think of it sometimes, the Truth.

I waited.

She looked at me. She seemed to analyze me. "You're an ex-cop, a witch, and a daemon," she said with careful enunciation.

"Yes. Daemons make very good witches, as you can imagine." I studied her, but I couldn't decide if she believed me or not. Probably not. "You can stay here, if you feel unsafe," I offered. "The Seraph cannot commit violence in a holy place, even if it's a pagan one. This place qualifies."

She gave me a guarded smile. She set the mug down and stood up. Her voice was very soft, neutral, carefully weighed. Mustn't upset the loony. "Thanks for the tea, Nick. I think I'll be going now, if you don't mind."

I had spooked her. I didn't think the Truth would set her free, but the idea of Malach hunting her—hurting her—because I hadn't warned her simply wasn't my thing. That was more than I could live with. I had to clear my own conscience. I had to try to help Vivian, especially if she was one of my own. I pulled my cell from my jeans pocket. "I'll call you a cab."

"I live eight blocks away, Nick. That big guy was probably just a freak looking for drugs."

I waited.

Vivian looked nervous. She didn't believe her own bullshit. She glanced down at the bloody hole she had picked in one thumbnail. "All right, fine, but I want to go home now." She no longer sounded calm. She sounded scared.

Before she left the loft, I gave her my cell number. I told her to call me anytime she was frightened, anytime she needed to talk. Day or night. I told her to seek a holy place if she felt hunted, a church, an occult shop, anything. Even a synagogue would do. Hopefully, she'd avoid Malach in the future. I didn't know if that was possible, but I was trying to be optimistic.

I didn't expect to hear from her again.

I was wrong. It's always the woman that changes your life, who makes it more interesting.

Like my life needs to be more interesting.

# | 2 |

WE OPEN THE shop at noon and close at midnight. Unless something unexpected comes up, or we have a client séance, Morgana takes the first shift from noon to six, and I watch the shop from six to twelve. Such are the hours of an occult shop. Morgana had tackled a séance the night before, so that meant it was my turn to do morning duty. But the following morning I'd overslept and woken around 11:45 to the sound of some very insistent pounding on the back door. I sat up in bed and flinched at the racket.

Morgana stirred and sat up beside me. She is tall and lanky, blonde like me. She keeps her weight strictly regulated with organic, non-meat products, yoga, and a daily five-mile jog. Meat, she says, interferes with her energies, as does my smoking and sarcasm.

I can only hope to be so energetic and focused when I'm Morgana's age. I smoke. I eat red meat. I like bagging girls. And guys, if they look like girls. Sue me. Morgana tells me that makes me a very bad witch, a very good daemon, and a typical male.

Morgana looked at me through gummy grey eyes and said, "Any chance you can get that, Nick? It's probably a delivery."

"The séance go badly?"

"Not at all. But Mr. Bingham brought company."

"Demons?"

"Some low-levels. Familiars, I think. But I cleaned house."

I lit a cigarette from the pack of Camels on the bedside table and sucked the smoke deep into my lungs. Morgana had succeeded in seriously pissing me off this morning. "You should have called me. You know I would have come."

She shrugged her thin shoulders. "There was a problem and I handled it."

"You don't handle demons. I do."

Morgana had gotten in at three o'clock in the morning looking like she'd been hit by a truck. I hadn't asked for details because I knew she would tell me given time, but I also hadn't known she'd been playing at being an amateur exorcist.

She'd held a circle for one of her aging clients, old Mrs. Bingham. The old woman had deep pockets and a great deal of guilt to unload on her newly deceased husband. I'm by nature a spiritual conduit. I certainly hadn't lied to Vivian about that. You'd think I'd be the man for the job, but I can't channel the dead. In fact, the dead don't come anywhere near me, not that I can blame them, really. The dead are pretty sensible chaps. The things I *can* communicate with are very much alive and have never been human. So Morgana had tackled the job for me while I stayed home watching a Lifetime movie marathon wherein I learned that all men are perverts, psychopaths, or both. Seriously, it was either that or old *Night Gallery* episodes, and I don't like it when art imitates my life.

See, if you need to speak to your dead mother, Morgana is the one you should call. If you need to speak to the low-level demon hiding in your child, well, I'm available three nights a week. Just saying.

"Nick..."

I threw back the covers, naked as the day I was born, the Camel clamped in my steel-trap jaw. Call it a point of contention, but I don't need Morgana doing my work for me. "I'm gonna go open up. I'm already late."

Morgana turned over to watch me dress in the dreary grey light of morning filtering through the one window. She's a witch, but still a woman, and she gets off on watching me dress, go figure.

"Don't be angry. I've been using tantric exercise to expand my powers."

I buttoned my jeans and turned to glance at her as I yanked last night's pullover back on. "And *that's* why you milked me the way you did last night."

"It was more exhausting than I'd anticipated."

"Which means you shouldn't be doing it yet."

"You are one crabby bastard in the morning, Scratch, do you know that?"

Then she smiled, and I smiled, and, as always, we forgave each other. I went over to her and pushed her long, mussed white-blonde hair aside and kissed her on the forehead. Like Malach, she and I have a history, just one that's a lot more enjoyable. I owe Morgana much. Well, everything, really.

She patted me companionably on the ass and told me I looked like hell and to get the patch already.

For the record, I don't have an actual romantic relationship with Morgana. We're very good friends with very good benefits, in more ways than you think. I naturally generate a great deal of ambient chaotic energy. Morgana has the unique ability to absorb and tune that energy. With it, she can increase her own magic exponentially for a short while, heal herself of injury, or restore her natural abilities after a particularly exhausting spiritual session, like last night. She can siphon the excess energy from me through either blood or sex. Sex is a great deal more fun than letting someone cut on you, let me tell you.

I wended my way down the back stairs, rubbing at my chin and throat. For a blondie like me, shaving is optional rather than a daily necessity. In any event, I figured if anyone complained about my unruly appearance today, I could just tell them I was rocking the Don Johnson look and hope to hell they were old enough to know what I was talking about. Maybe after tea I'd change my mind, shave nicely, dress better, and stop smoking. Not likely, but hope springs ever eternal, at least according to Morgana.

In the delivery alley behind the shop, I found three parcels waiting for me, all bearing return labels from our supplier in Salem. They weren't heavy, but I was still obviously in recoup mode. As I lifted them, my nerves jumped slightly under my skin as if I'd been beaten with Nerf bats for a good long time. Morgana had said I was positively humming with energy last night, overflowing with it. She'd pushed me down onto the bed, climbed on top of me, and milked me for a good twenty minutes, until my eyes had rolled up in my head and I had started speaking in tongues, literally. Then she wanted to know who Vivian was.

I knew I should probably tell her, just not right now. It was possible that Vivian would never call, never enter my life again, and there would be no need to mention her. The thought was fatally depressing as I set the parcels on the counters in the back room and started on the tape with a utility knife. Behind me, through the open door, I could smell autumn—fertility wilting, that damp, warm rush of leaves and apples and the promise of cold rains that just makes you want to sleep all day. I left the door open to air out the cinnamon incense in the back room, and just because I love the scent of fall in the mountains.

I don't get out nearly enough, despite living in the center of backpacking and camping central. It helps to have someone to go with, I suppose. I wondered if Vivian was into kayaking, camping—all the things New Yorkers swarmed this town for on weekends.

Highly imaginative thoughts of Vivian were busily lifting my spirits when I heard someone knock on the open door. I turned to find Blackwater's own Sheriff Ben Oswell standing there with a foam cup full of nitro java from NiBor's.

"Ben. How goes it?" I asked.

"It goes, Nick," he said, watching me attack the boxes.

Ben's in his early forties like me, but a whole hell of a lot more ambitious, and nothing like your typical small-town sheriff type. He's not greedy, fat, sloppy, or corrupt. I mean, I can't say for certain that his computer at home isn't full of llama porn, for instance, or that he doesn't cheat on his taxes, but I know he doesn't take bribes, and he doesn't bang college coeds. He has a wife his own age, a daughter who stays out of trouble, a dog, and an arrowhead collection. That's saying a lot in this town.

Ben is tall, dark, and as lean as a totem, without an inch of fat anywhere. He has a predilection for mirrored sunglasses and gourmet coffee. He doesn't suffer fools gladly. All leftovers from his days with the state troopers. Ben had an African-American dad and a Shawnee mom. I've seen Ben express Synchronicity on occasion, the innate supernatural ability to be in the right place at the right time, but I still haven't figured out if that's because of his mom or his dad. Ben hates his mojo, and mine, but he's not above using it to get the job done. I do respect that about the man.

He looked into one of the boxes sitting on the counter. "Well, that's awful ugly. What are those?"

"Hopi kachina dolls," I explained as I grabbed a mug off the counter, filled it with tap water from the basin sink, and stuck it in the microwave for two minutes. "Effigies made of cottonwood that embody the ceremonial kachina. You want one?"

"If I brought something like that home my dog would eat it or my wife would eBay it."

"That would be very bad sorcery for you," I said in my wisest occult shopkeeper's voice.

"What are you supposed to do with it, anyway?"

I dug out one in eagle dress with its feathered arms outstretched. "You sit and think on it."

"Just think on it."

I offered it to him. "This one represents good fortune in seeking lost items. Pretty fitting for a policeman, in my opinion."

He took it and looked it over. When he found the price tag, he lurched a bit. "Shit, I can't afford to think that hard, Nick. Why can't you just sell Webkinz like everyone else in this town?"

He started handing the kachina back to me, but I shook my head.

"Keep it. When I saw it, I knew it was yours. That it was waiting for you."

He looked at me steadily, and even though I couldn't see his eyes past his Super Trooper shades, I knew he was shaken. He didn't believe in mojo, but he also couldn't leave it alone. "You are one spooky bastard, you know that, Nick?" But he slid the kachina dutifully into his pocket. He once told me it was against Shawnee custom to refuse a gift.

The microwave beeped and I got my water out, added a tea bag, and picked up the third as yet unopened parcel. With it stuffed securely under my arm and my tea in hand, I turned to the beaded curtain. "Don't mind me; I'm late with opening the shop."

Ben took a sip of coffee and followed me out onto the floor. "The Berger girl is missing."

I set the box on the counter and turned to look at him. "The Bergers of Berger Hollow?"

"That's them. You know 'em?"

"Not really," I said, going to the door and unlocking it. There wasn't exactly a line, though I knew Morgana had some longtime clients dropping by later today to pick up some elixirs. "I know the family name, one of the Blackwater founders, correct?" Actually, I knew that to be true. Our humble little mountain burg had been settled at a crossroads by four founding families, the Kings, the Rinkleys, the Bergers and the Wodehouses, though the Bergers and Wodehouses were nearly extinct now.

Ben nodded.

"I didn't know they had a girl."

"Most people don't. She's sick, the girl. Has special needs."

I nodded my head in that *ahh* way you do when you really have no idea what to say. I slid behind the counter as the first customer stepped into the shop. It was a bored-looking tourist, not a local, which relieved me some. That meant she'd likely browse for a while before finding something. The cop in me wanted to hear Ben's story.

"Cassandra Berger disappeared from her home between one and two yesterday afternoon," Ben said. He consulted his notepad. Like any good cop, he wanted his facts straight. "The father, Thom Berger, was at work. His wife Rebecca was home, but she was downstairs doing laundry. The girl vanished from their backyard. Rebecca reported it immediately. We canvassed the whole neighborhood, but no one saw anything. We're organizing a search team later today to search the woods behind the house. The Bergers' house is butted right up against the bottom of Bear Mountain."

I sat down behind the counter. There were about a hundred things wrong with this whole scenario and my sarcasm just jumped out of me. "Because leaving a disabled girl alone in the backyard is a truly excellent idea."

Ben put the notepad away. "If the Bergers screwed up, I'll be more than happy to put their asses in the system, believe me." He watched me light a new smoke in that hungry way he had. He'd been on the patch for six months. So much for the patch. "You wanna help with Search and Rescue? Because we sure could use it. There's about five miles of woods going back."

"Depends on whether the Kings will be there, I guess."

"A third of the town is turning out for this, Nick. I ain't promising anything, and I ain't refereeing."

I waved the smoke away and thought about that. Two years ago, Ben asked me to help his boys bushwhack Indian Mountain Lakes Park where a lone hiker had gone missing for six days. Turned out, he'd stumbled upon the remnants of an old house that had burned down years ago and he'd gone right through the crumbling floorboards, winding up in a dry septic tank with a broken ankle. The sulfur residue from the septic tank had confused the tracker dogs and he was too weak to make much noise. God knows what he ate or drank. Or maybe God had no idea. Wouldn't surprise me much. I found him alive, but only after I'd left my particular group. Bradley King, who qualified as red, white, and blue—redneck, blue collar, with white sheets hanging in his closet—wouldn't stop aiming his gun at me and talking with his Saturday night fight club friends about adding a New Age fag to the collection of stuffed animals in his den.

Every town has a walking cliché. We have Bradley King.

I ran a hand through my hair. The tourist looked over from the bookshelves and gave me a disapproving look. My last haircut had left me with scruffy 1980s David Bowie hair. She probably thought I was an alcoholic, chain-smoking transient being picked over by the police and was wondering where the real owner was.

I really didn't want to go stomping through woods until I found some half-eaten girl a bear had buried under a tree while a bunch of rednecks had a tailgating party. Not my idea of a good time. Yet the cop in me was already dumping loads of guilt onto my conscience. "What time?" I finally asked.

"As soon as you can get away. We started organizing this morning."

"I'll see if I can get Morgana to cover."

"Thanks, Nick." Ben actually smiled a little before he left the shop.

The tourist, an older lady who looked a bit like one of those church ladies you see who has ten cats, checked out two books, an embroidered scarf, and some Navajo earrings. Before she left she said, "You know, I don't believe in any of this New Age stuff. God is the only way, the truth and the light." She set a tract down, one more to add to my ever-growing collection. "Why don't you come back to Jesus, young man?"

I smiled nicely. In retail, the customer is always right. "His dad and my dad don't get along, I'm afraid."

The church lady left the shop looking very confused.

# | 3 |

I BIKED OUT to the Berger house at the end of Berger Hollow Road. The weather was balmy cool and simply too nice to stuff myself into a car. Besides, the Bergers lived in a development only two miles away, and I'll do anything to save a few cents on the ridiculous cost of gas these days. The car I owned was a huge Dodge Monaco and it hoarded oil like an Arabian sheik.

The Bergers, though among the first settlers in the area, were a dying breed, and Thom Berger was the last of his kind, so far as I knew. The family had taken a massive hit during the Depression and never really recovered. They'd started out as city elders but wound up lawyers and business owners.

By the time I got down to the development where the last of the Bergers lived, the tailgating party was in full swing. The Bergers lived in a huge neo-Colonial that looked only a few years old, brick-faced, with two wings. The lawn, even this late in the season, was a chemically treated, eye-sizzling green, and there were planters full of yellow and rust-colored mums in the window boxes. The long, curving asphalt drive was crammed with vehicles, mostly huge blue pickups covered in decals. In Blackwater, it's mandatory to own two things: 1. a dark blue 4x4 with decals; and 2. a red and blue Phillies cap. That's in the manual somewhere. Those who couldn't fit their monster truck in the drive had parked it on the lawn, and I could imagine the lawn guy having conniption fits when he saw the big muddy furrows when next he did the Bergers' lawn.

Behind the Berger house rose a panoramic view of Bear Mountain, so big it looked sheer going straight up, a misty fairytale blue that was one of the perks of living this close to the Blue Ridge Mountain Range.

The tailgates on all the blue 4x4s were down and the locals were hyping themselves. I saw plenty of plastic Igloo coolers and Tupperware full of cold food being expertly handled by pretty, manicured wives. There was a lot of beer being manhandled. A scattering of hounds bayed nervously from inside truck cabs. I froze momentarily and attempted to prepare myself for stepping into this particular hornets' nest.

Brad King and his boys were gathered around his giant blue Cadillac Escalade. Brad stood outside with his elbow resting in the open window as Toby Keith bellowed soulfully about the red, white, and blue. Meanwhile, his bleached-blonde wife ran in circles around him, a cell phone clipped to her ear, unloading the flatbed. Brad spotted me immediately like he had radar tuned in to just witches, then turned and said something to a member of his Legion of Doom while flopping his wrist rather dramatically. The Legion of Doom member snickered in response.

Boys and girls, inbreeding is bad.

I sighed, crushed out my cigarette, stuck my hands in my belted trench coat, and ambled forward, edging toward the police vehicles parked in the street.

"Hey, it's Dick Tracy," one of Ben's deputies said, looking up from a thick manual he was reading in the midst of all this chaos. Did the police actually have to consult a manual on how to canvass a wooded area? He was young, early twenties, and probably wouldn't know Dick Tracy from a hole in the ground.

I ignored him and looked around, spotting Ben heading toward me. I wondered if he still had the kachina doll in his pocket.

"Nick," he said, "thanks for showing up." He did that guy slap thing on my shoulder and handed me a photocopied Google grid map that meant almost nothing to me. Telling a New Yorker to go north *here* or south *there* rather than *right* or *left* is about as helpful as teaching a pig to sing. I crumpled the map up in my pocket as he started giving me a rundown of the procedure. There were going to be fifty-four teams, two per every hundred feet. We were going to fan out, heading north to Cherry Hill, the next big town over. He hadn't known who to buddy me up with, so I was going with Deputy Dog. Oh joy. Still better than getting one of the members of the Legion of Doom, I suppose. He'd likely shoot me in the woods and claim I looked like a deer.

"Are those the grieving parents?" I said, nodding discreetly toward the back of the house. A couple stood there talking to a reporter from Mountaintop Radio, our local talk station. I recognized the reporter, Shelley Preston, the shining, young face of modern daytime talk radio. She had that perky palomino beach bunny look you normally associate with Venice Beach gurus and reruns of *Baywatch*, her skin carefully spray-tanned four shades darker than her long golden tresses.

Four years ago, while Shelley was working for a minor local paper, she visited Curiosities and interviewed me for their Halloween edition, hoping to gain insight on the local pagan establishments. At least, that's what she told me. While we were alone in the loft, she nearly bit my dick off. She reacted badly to me throwing her out. The following day, Shelley's paper ran a piece debunking everything that Curiosities did. Morgana was livid. She cast a spell on Shelley and the girl lost all her hair for a month. That was the day I learned an abiding respect for Morgana's power.

So I had Brad King on one side and Shelley Preston on the other. I was starting to feel like Odysseus trying to navigate between Scylla and Charybdis.

"That's the Bergers, yeah," Ben said, not looking at them. His attention kept coming back around to Shelley, as any red-blooded American man's would. I wasn't about to judge him; I just didn't agree with his tastes in women. Shelley had that perfected Hollywood beauty that I personally find rather bland. She looked like any of a hundred popular leading actresses. Not to mention, she didn't have the natural curves I favor. Not that I'm stuck on curves. Really.

The Bergers, on the other hand, were very much natives of the northeast Pennsylvanian mountains, with ancestry dating back generations, at least. The husband, Thom Berger, was tall and stoop-shouldered and perfectly bald, like someone had greased his head and then shaved it clean. He wore glasses. His wife was only half as tall and had plump, baby doll arms poking out of a sleeveless white halter top that she was just a hair too old to be wearing. She too wore glasses, and her limp, standard-issue dark blonde hair was tied into a ponytail. She looked in her mid-twenties. Her husband looked closer to fifty. Not that I'm one to judge. I mean, as far as I'm concerned, as long as it's legal and consensual, do as thou wilt shall be the whole of the law. Still, there's something uber-creepy about cradle-robbers, and as an itch started between my shoulder blades, I realized I immediately disliked Thom Berger.

I watched him gesture wildly to Shelley as he spoke, though his wife looked zonked, a blonde zombie in a halter top. I hoped the Xanax trip was being good to her.

"Can I talk to the couple?" I asked Ben rather suddenly. I was getting the same feeling off the couple as with Vivian, only inverted. Instead of empowered, I was feeling slightly weakened.

Ben looked surprised, but not really put off. If I was just a citizen, I knew he wouldn't have allowed it. But I was a cop—ex-cop—and

I was here doing him a favor. He sort of had to let me. He directed his two deputies to start assembling the search teams, then turned back to me. "Is this about going with Branson?"

I assumed Branson was Deputy Dog. "No," I said, looking away back toward the Bergers. "I just want to talk to them, satisfy a curiosity."

"You gonna do mojo on them?"

I smiled. Mojo wasn't what I had in mind, and even if it was, I wasn't sure what kind of mojo would help me find a lost child, but if Ben wanted to believe that, so be it.

In the end, he let me approach the Bergers while the search parties started bushwhacking around the back of the house. The Bergers looked at me with deer-in-the-headlights eyes as I approached. I have that effect on some folks. Ben escorted me, saying, "Mr. and Mrs. Berger, this is Nick Englebrecht. I asked him to be here today. He's a psychic detective."

Ben was using the soft voice you use to calm frightened horses. I tried for an approximation because normally I sound like I'm gargling razor blades.

"Mr. and Mrs. Berger," I said, shaking Mr. Berger's hand. Despite his impressive height, my hand entirely enveloped his. Thom Berger looked at it, and I thought of that old wives' tale—small hands and feet means equally small equipment. I have large hands and feet, just in case you're wondering. Mrs. Berger stared at me and through me like I wasn't there.

"You're a real detective?" Thom Berger said. He looked me over skeptically. I guess the Dick Tracy trench coat hadn't won him over.

"I'm retired but I do odd jobs for Ben." Not the actual truth, but close enough to pass. "Can we go inside for a moment?"

The Bergers' kitchen was pristine white and blue. The tile gleamed and there were spotless pots and pans hanging over an island large enough to do the Watusi down. It had a glistening magazine-layout look that suggested that the Bergers ate out a lot. That, or they had a terrific maid. Thom led us to one of those breakfast nook thingies that look like they belong in a high-end restaurant and said, "I'm afraid I gave Zanita the day off. Can I get you gentlemen anything? Coffee?" His eyes flicked nervously over us and he flinched when he moved. I hate flinchy people.

"Tea, if you have it," I said.

"I only have coffee, I'm afraid," Thom said, indicating the coffeepot that I'm sure his underpaid Mexican housekeeper had set up earlier today. I was going into cliché overload here.

I waved my hand. "Pass."

Ben took a coffee and I got out the notebook I normally use to mark down incoming shipments to the shop. On his way back to us with Ben's coffee, Thom said, again sounding flinchy, "You sure you don't want a coffee, Mr. Englebrecht? I thought that was all cops drank?"

"I used to drink it," I told him.

"What happened?"

"I saw my partner killed in front of me. I can't stomach the stuff anymore."

Thom looked at me blankly. He had no idea what to say to that. Good.

I said, "Can you tell me in detail what happened to little Cassandra?"

Thom looked at his wife, sitting on the edge of the booth and staring fixedly at her fingers where her nail polish was rubbing off. "I've been over all this with Sheriff Oswell already."

"But not me," I said.

He looked over at Ben, who nodded. "Tell him, Thom. He does know his stuff…even if he is a little spooky looking."

Thom locked eyes with me and we shared a moment of profound dislike. Then he told me pretty much the same story that Ben had told me earlier. When we got to Cassandra's disability, I interrupted. "How do you spell that?" I asked, and dutifully wrote down *Tay-Sachs Disease* in the notebook for later Googling. I had never heard of it before.

"It's a neurological disorder that prevents Cassandra from walking or speaking," Thom explained. "She has to be hand fed, bathed, and carried."

"She's five years old?"

"That's correct."

"So there's no chance she wandered off? Crawled off, maybe?"

"Cassie can't crawl," the mother, Rebecca Berger said, suddenly coming alive. Her voice was soft but focused. "She can't do anything without help. I know someone took her, I just know it!" She glared at me as if this were somehow my fault.

"Rebecca," Thom said softly. "He's trying to help."

"Then why isn't he out there helping?" she barked.

I ignored her outburst. I wasn't about to take a mother who had just lost her only child to task. I looked down at my notes instead. "Cassie requires almost constant care?"

"Yes," Thom Berger answered, though his voice was more guarded now.

"Do you have any enemies, Mr. Berger? Anyone who might want to do you or Mrs. Berger harm?"

Thom Berger looked angry. "I run a True Value, Mr. Englebrecht. You don't make many enemies selling weather seal."

"Is there anyone in your past who might want to harm you or your wife?" I repeated.

"No one."

"Have you noticed anyone new in the neighborhood? Anyone—anything—suspicious or out of the ordinary?"

"Nothing," he answered, his voice cold and dead. I could tell that Thom Berger didn't think much of psychic detectives.

Ten minutes later, I was standing in the backyard, looking over the area where Cassie Berger used to sit and play. A privacy fence ran the whole backyard. There was a swing set and a sandbox and a safe plastic slide. There were toys scattered around, some Barbies, and a plastic bucket and shovel for the sandbox. One of the Barbies was lying in the sandbox, half buried. I picked it up. It was a holiday angel Barbie. I moved to the swing set. It was sturdy, built to last for generations like the ones in the orphanages where I'd grown up. Everything in the backyard had been dusted down for fingerprints. Only Cassie and her parents' had been found. I sat down on the seat of the swing and looked out toward the far side of the backyard, the Barbie in my lap.

A few minutes later, Ben appeared beside me. "Good questions," he said. Up on the mountain, someone shot off a shotgun and he sighed and shook his head. The natives were restless and ready to play. "What were you digging for?"

I shrugged. "Sometimes the way they answer is more important than the answer itself." I thought about that. "Does Thom Berger regularly dope his wife, or is this just a special occasion?"

"She takes Zoloft for anxiety and depression."

"Ah."

"You think she did her own kid in?"

I shrugged. "There's a theory."

I stood up and walked to the gate. Like everything else, it had been dusted already. There was a latch on it, not exactly childproof, but far enough up that I was pretty certain a five-year-old couldn't reach it, even if she'd been able to crawl the length of the backyard. Something more was going on. Something bad.

I stepped out into the woods with the doll under my arm.

## | 4 |

TWO YEARS AGO, I found the lost hiker, but I hadn't found him alone. Brownswick had helped me.

I wondered if he would help me find Cassie Berger, assuming she was still in the woods. Then again, I'd left him pissed off the last time I'd seen him. Maybe he would just kick me in the nuts and stomp off. He wouldn't be the first. I know Morgana wanted to kick me after I got her out of bed to watch the shop this morning. Over the years, I've developed a rather long kicking list among both my allies and enemies. I'm just lucky that way.

Brownswick is my animal familiar. Every witch has at least one. Morgana has crows, the most populous creature in this part of the state. They're beautiful and scary, and she can even see through their eyes. They don't talk, or talk back. I have fauns and satyrs, who do. No, really. I definitely got the short straw, in my opinion.

I didn't go looking for Brownswick this time, either. Brownswick came to me. I had only hiked perhaps three-quarters of the way into the woods, up a steep incline, and through enough blue firs to cover my coat in needles, when I noticed him. You don't *see* fauns; you notice them. Or rather, they *let* you notice them. Brownswick was seated in the boughs of one of the aforementioned blue firs, eating a honeycomb while a swarm of angry honeybees surrounded him. They were likely stinging him, though Brownswick didn't notice, or else didn't care, though he did scratch at one of his ears with a foreleg before glancing down at me. "Hello, my Lord, have you returned to pay the piper?"

"I don't have to pay you for your services, Brownie," I reminded him. "You live to serve me, remember?"

"I serve you now. But one day I will serve my Lord's purposes no longer." He smiled down at me, a secret smile full of wisdom and sadness, perhaps malice. It's hard to tell with fauns. "What need have you with me when you will one day have the world at your feet?"

"The world is overrated. I shall always need my Brownie."

"You have a sweet tongue, Little Horn. Perhaps you will lend it to me. I should like to suck it like a honeycomb." He landed almost soundlessly on his hooves without even disturbing the bough of the tree he'd been perched in. He glared at me, challenging me to run. Faun 101: It's very important you *never* run from a faun after one reveals itself to you. Fauns love a good chase through the woods. It whets their appetite.

Brownswick is huge and lank. He towers over even me, which is saying a lot. He has thick, muscular elken legs and hooves sharp enough to rip human flesh from bone. I found myself staring at his chest rather than his face, where some Greek pipes hung from a rope of rose vines twined around his neck. His face is young and beautiful, deceptively innocent, the face of a stud on the front cover of a romance novel. The last time I had seen him, he had been in velvet, with short, blunt antlers. Those had grown into an enormous, sprawling rack of sharp, ebony antlers big enough to lift a whole man into the air. More rose vines were entangled in them, with some bees and butterflies flitting about. Very prosaic until you saw the size of his wang. Let's just say, fauns represent the dark side of nature. Deer found ripped apart in these woods are not always the victim of flesh-eating predators. His fur was darker, courser, and his musk was enough to give me a migraine headache. I was fairly certain he was in full stag.

I lit a cigarette to cut the smell and to keep him at bay with the smoke. A faun in stag is not the safest thing to be around. They will rut with literally *anything*. Thankfully, they also hate all things manmade, cigarettes being on the top of their list. See, smoking does have its benefits.

"The son of perdition seeks the son of the forest." Brownswick made a tutting noise of disapproval. He pissed against the side of the tree I was leaning on. "Yet you do not visit me in idleness. This makes me sad, my Lord."

I shifted away from the faun piss, checking to make certain Brownie hadn't gotten any on my coat. "I'm wondering if you've seen a girl in the forest. I'm looking for her."

"Is she beautiful, this maiden you've lost?"

I uncrumpled the map I'd stuck in my coat pocket. On the backside, the police department had photocopied a picture of Cassandra Berger for the search party. Underneath the picture were her stats. I showed Brownswick the picture. "She's five years old. Have you seen her?"

Brownswick looked the picture over with very little interest, then turned his head and *whuffed* like a horse at my clothes. He smiled. "My Lord, you have been with a female of your own kind!" he announced with enormous satisfaction. "Will you be rutting with her?"

Well, that proved what Vivian was, as if I had any doubts. Brownswick would know. I looked up at the faun who was practically looming over me, glaring at me in his usual feral way. His tail twitched, and I wondered what was going through his little faun brain, not that I wanted to know.

"I have no idea what I'll be doing with her, Brownie."

"I know." Brownswick grinned. He had huge, faintly sharp teeth. "I see the future sometimes in the still waters. She will be your kryptonite, my lord."

"You need to stop eavesdropping on campers, Brownie," I said. "Your slang is terrible."

"That does not make it untrue."

"What about the little girl?"

"The girl is of no interest to me. She is obviously not of an age to rut."

"Have you seen her?" I shoved the picture in his face. He lurched back, his hooves stomping the damp, leafy ground. I knew that the hoofmarks left behind would look exactly like those of a gigantic stag, and no hunter in these woods would be any the wiser. A part of me—an evil part, I admit—imagined Brad King lusting after the rack of the stag that left such marks year after endless year, but never finding it. A man's gotta have his fantasies.

"I do not know," Brownswick said at last.

"How can you not know? This entire mountain is your territory."

Brownswick shook his head and his massive antlers grazed the low branches of the tree we stood beneath, me with my back to the trunk, Brownie practically pinning me to it. I thought the weight of them had to be substantial. I wondered how he managed to keep his head up. "I have been with my nymphs these past few days, my Lord. It is the season to rut. I have not set foot in the forest for almost three days."

"Such a Romeo, Brownie."

"You, my Lord, are jealous." He smiled at me in a lascivious way.

I smiled back, not to be outdone. "You're probably right. Will you keep the picture and let me know if you see her?" I knew I was asking a lot. Just touching a manmade piece of paper was a great sacrifice on Brownswick's part. Then I remembered the doll. "And will you take this as well? It belonged to the girl and probably still carries her scent."

He took these things gingerly between his clawed fingers as if he might be infected by them. "If it pleases you. I will ask the nymphs to look as well."

"I appreciate that."

"My wives will be much more interested in finding the girl than I," he warned me. "I seek other pursuits." Brownie drew close to my face and I thought I might gag on the smell of him. "And you have still not paid the piper, daemon. I expect payment from the other-creatures who cross my woods, even if they *are* my lord."

"Sorry, I didn't bring my checkbook."

The faun drew back and stamped at the ground angrily, kicking up a fury of small stones. "Run, daemon."

"No," I told him steadily, blowing a smoke ring at Brownie. "I don't think so." As a creature only half-human, I wasn't protected under the natural Laws that prevented human beings from being hunted by the other-creatures. What all that translated into was: *A lot of weird shit could come after me.* Not that I was going to let that worry me. Much.

It occurred to me that Vivian was in just as much danger as I, especially from these woods.

Brownswick smiled again, as if he were reading my thoughts in his naughty way. "I sense my Lord will soon be in rut as well. Perhaps you and the female daemon will return to these woods then. I should like to meet the future queen of perdition. I should like to know her."

"I bet you would," I told him.

"You must pay me *something*. It is my right. I am king here."

I reached into my pocket and gave the faun a melty yellow pack of peanut M&Ms I'd been carrying around with me for some while.

"See ya, Brownie." I left him to go explore the woods.

* * *

I moved west toward Cherry Hill, through the sun-speckled forest, watching my step as I clambered over the brambly, leaf-littered ground full of roots and soft sinkholes. I wondered about those horror movies where the psychotic killer pursues some busty female victim for miles through the nighttime woods. I would have gotten about five hundred feet before I fell off the mountain. I don't think Hollywood filmmakers have *ever* been in deep woods, at least not like these where it's as dark as night even at noontime and everything snags your clothes.

I was alone in this neck of the woods. I could hear the occasional blast a few miles off as the tailgating party shot at squirrels and rabbits. Otherwise, the woods were quiet. Much too quiet. I didn't even hear the cry of crows, and there are *always* crows around somewhere.

Eventually I found an old Indian trail. It wended through some close stands of maple trees and white paper birch. The tall grasses and vegetation were stamped flat in some places. I could tell it had been used recently, maybe by hikers, maybe by something else. The grasses were green and broken. Hey, I may be a city mouse, but I know how to track. *CSI* and Animal Planet, you know? I followed the trail for a mile or so until I reached the edge of a ravine. It angled sharply downward where it met a narrow creek with rocky sides. Beyond that was a cagey tree area that looked almost pitch black, what the locals call a *hollow*. I'd been walking for about an hour and a half. I knew by the number of cigarettes I had smoked. You can either admire that or let it horrify you. I don't care either way.

I scrambled down the side of the ravine, my insulated Skechers kicking up a lot of dirt and rocks. A jackrabbit bounded out of my way. Compared to Brownie, I probably had the grace of a water buffalo. Then again, I didn't prance around the woods all day with my harem of nymphs.

I ducked down and the hollow closed over me like a cave. It felt like midnight underneath the dense canopy of trees—mostly pine and big, frothy firs. It was also cold as hell and smelled deeply of tree sap, dry needles, and wild animal urine. I think my New York senses revolted at the lack of pollution. I slapped at the mosquitoes trying to land on my face.

I decided I didn't want to be here. There was a huge feeling of *keep out* that kept tickling along my spine and making my stomach turn over. So of course I needed to go on. I found myself clomping along the needle-strewn earth, moving like I was in a suspicious warehouse somewhere on the Eastside, my silver Tanaka Smith & Wesson n my hand, my finger on the safety. I didn't remember drawing the gun.

The Tanaka is a hand cannon, larger than a Desert Eagle and somewhat similar in design to Dirty Harry's gun. It's sexy as hell and can take down a bear. I've had it since the force but I hadn't chosen it to feel macho. The other police-issue Glocks and S&Ws just didn't fit my big hands right. I wondered what I planned on doing with it should I encounter something untoward in the deep woods. Even the Tanaka's .50 caliber rounds only had a fifty-fifty chance of taking down something supernatural, depending on where I shot it.

I stopped when I reached the weird patch. I'm not sure what else to call it. The golden-brown needles of the firs that had completely littered the ground were sparser here in a roughly rectangular area maybe twenty feet wide by fifty feet long. I could see the wet, packed earth as it squelched around my hiking boots. I might have worried.

Missing child plus churned earth equals tragedy, if you know what I mean. Still, this wasn't recent—not recent enough, anyway. The earth had been disturbed some time back, at the beginning of the summer, maybe.

One way to make certain.

I got down on my knees, slid the Tanaka back into its armpit holster, and started digging up clumps of wet heavy soil with my hands. Not a wholly pleasant experience. Thankfully, it wasn't hard. We'd had some good rains the last few days and the earth was loose. If this were the height of summer, I would have needed a jackhammer.

About a foot down, I hit something. I scraped aside the earth and recognized it as a shoebox. Pretty obvious, since it was pink and said *Candies* on the part I was looking at.

I dug down and squirmed it loose. The moment of truth, boys and girls. If there was a body part in the box, I was going to close it up, find Ben, and hand it to him to deal with. I ripped away the frayed hemp and knocked the lid off. Inside was tissue paper, and under that...a doll. That was better than a bloody finger, I supposed.

The doll was made of gingham cloth, hand sewn, with just two small button eyes for a face. Small cloth wings were sewn to it. So it was an angel doll...thingy. I wrapped it in the tissue paper and slipped it into my pocket. I put the shoebox back the way I'd found it and covered up the hole I'd dug. I tried another random spot, with the same results. Another shoebox. Inside was another angel doll. Whereas the one in my pocket was blue gingham, this one was red. I tried one more spot and...you guessed it. Another shoebox. The angel doll in this one was yellow gingham.

I stood up, a demon with a pocket full of angels, enjoying the irony of that, somehow. I had no idea what the angels meant, if anything. The angels might contain something of monetary value, like little Maltese Falcons. Or they could be weapons in a huge spiritual battle. Or the angels could be just angels, in shoeboxes, buried in the ground. I'd have to ask Morgana's advice.

They were pretty cute, the little angels. Couldn't be anything too sinister.

Right?

| 5 |

BEN CALLED IN the search party at five, when it started getting dark. No point to having the locals stumbling around the woods at night and getting lost.

No one had found any trace of Cassandra Berger. Herb Rinkley, a close associate of Brad King, fell over a log and fractured his ankle. Charlotte Bearsely, who had turned out along with her wife Meg Maguire, got into a pushing match with Brad King, who called her a diesel dyke. The two wound up exchanging blows and rolling around the forest floor until Deputy Branson separated them. Branson cited Charlotte for public indecency. Holly King, Brad's eldest daughter, threw up in a thatch of wild thistle. They said it was either her mother's coleslaw or she was knocked up. Four people caught poison ivy, one poison sumac, and all the victims were dutifully rushed to the emergency room. Shelley interviewed several members of the Search and Rescue team and everyone made their ordeal out to be an episode of *Survivor*. Seven squirrels were shot, and two jackrabbits. One person claimed to see a chupacabra. That was pretty much the excitement for the day.

Exhausted from my hike, I biked back to Curiosities. When I reached the shop, I found Morgana selling old Mrs. Bailey some herbs for her arthritis. Mrs. Bailey is actually a completely awesome person. She stood at the counter, dressed primly in a bright, flowery dress and honest-to-God gloves and a hat. Mrs. Bailey did not believe in leaving the house without looking like a proper lady. She was one of the few people in Blackwater who did not spook at my appearance, though I couldn't have blamed her if she had. When I walked into the shop, I was covered head to toe in dirt and sweat from my pleasant little hike over Bear Mountain. My hair was spiky with sweat, and there were scratches and bug bites on my cheeks. I probably looked like I hadn't shaved in two weeks. I wondered how people who backpacked and camped regularly in the mountains managed to pull it off without coming out of the woods looking like Sasquatch.

"Nicky!" Mrs. Bailey said, giving me her usual dazzling smile. "What have you done to yourself?"

"I tried to backpack."

"Tried?"

"I flunked," I said, snorting because there was pollen and dirt up my nose. "Those mountains are brutal to us city folks."

Mrs. Bailey laughed. "I was telling Miss Morgana about Mr. Phipps. He was barking at the attic stairs again." She paused dramatically. "It's very unusual for him to be doing that. Do you think I could have a ghost?"

"Well, your house is very old," I said. I had learned long ago that trying to reason with Mrs. Bailey about her high-strung, inbred Pomeranian was useless. People like Mrs. Bailey spent their whole lives hoping to meet a ghost or demon. I spend mine trying to avoid them. Unfortunately, the supernatural sticks to me like shit on a baby's blanket. "Did you want me to come out and take a look around later this week?"

"Would you?"

"Of course." The worse that could happen was that I'd come back laden with Mrs. Bailey's most excellent apple butter.

After Mrs. Bailey left, Morgana gave me a funny look. She stood behind the counter in one of her sheer, flowy lavender gowns, big gold half-moon earrings dangling from her ears. She looked like a very beautiful gypsy...except for the frown on her face.

"She's an old woman," I said with a shrug as I set the angel dolls in their tissue paper down on the counter. "What can it hurt?"

I unwrapped the angel dolls. "Any chance you can take a look at these? Maybe identify them? They might be nothing, or maybe some kind of talisman. I'm not sure."

Morgana glared at me.

"Look, what's the deal about Mrs. Bailey?"

"Not that. *That*." She pointed at the floor where I'd tracked in some muddy footprints. Then she turned to the backroom and I swear to God a mop just flew into her hands. She handed it over to me. "Clean it up, Mr. Wizard."

\* \* \*

After I'd cleaned the shop, I showered, shaved, and put my muddy, Brownswick-musky clothes in a laundry bag—I couldn't decide if I should wash them or burn them. Then I changed into a woolly white pullover and a fresh pair of jeans and, looking human again, went down to relieve Morgana for the night. There were more customers than usual, mostly locals looking for little additions to their upcoming Samhain and Halloween parties later this month. I made a note in the ledger we keep in the kneehole to order additional Ouija boards and black candles. They seemed to be selling out.

Around eight o'clock, Morgana swept back into the shop. She was wearing a very becoming while silk dress with Celtic embroidery around the sleeves and collar. Her long silvery blonde hair was crimped and glittering and she wore her favorite rose crystal around her neck.

I wolf-whistled. "Hot date?"

"Anton is taking me to the Old Opera House. Clannad's on tour," she told me. She leaned over the counter and wrote down the hours she expected to be gone. It had become a routine with us. Our safety net, so to speak. At eleven, when the concert was over, she'd leave a message on my cell if she planned to spend the night at Anton's. I did the same for her. Sadly, Morgana was leaving many more messages on my phone than I was on hers.

"You and Anton getting pretty serious?" I leaned on the counter and cradled my cheek as I talked to her. Call it brotherly concern, but I liked to keep track of who was keeping time with Morgana. She did the same for me. That way, we knew who to hex next.

She shook her head, her half-moon earrings flashing. "I'm not sure, to be honest. He's nice enough. Older."

Anton McGinley was the high priest of the Morristown coven, a nice enough fellow if you liked dry academics with receding hairlines in tweed and glasses.

"You're just spoiled, being with a stud like me," I teased.

"Maybe," she said with a deep grin. She leaned in close so I could smell her flowery shampoo. She looked deep into my eyes. "You have that whole scruffy, burned-out detective thing going on, Nick. It's hard for guys to compete with that."

"Prince of Darkness. Don't forget that."

"As if I could." She kissed my cheek and tousled my hair. "At least you shaved." She picked up her purse, settled it on her shoulder, and started for the door, then stopped. "Oh...I researched the dolls and marked the pages in the books upstairs. Take a read. Some interesting things."

After Morgana left, some punks came in and started going through the DVDs, disappointed to find no horror movies or porn.

Then they stepped up to the counter and asked to see the wands in the open box in the display case. "You got any like Harry Potter?" one of the punks asked.

I showed them the wands. "They're not toys," I warned.

"So they do actual magic?" the one girl with them asked with genuine interest.

"They only do what you want them to do," I told her. "No more, no less."

The boy with her who had his hand in the ass-pocket of her jeans, said, "You a real magician?"

"Criss Angel is a magician. I'm a witch."

"A real witch?" The kid challenging me smiled slyly, crookedly. "If you were a *real* witch you'd know I'd taken something from your shop."

"The blue crystal in your back pocket," I told him. I smiled and narrowed my eyes at him until he flinched. I can do the whole Prince of Darkness thing when I need to. "And if you don't pay for it, the penis in your pants—which, by the way, you stuff out with a sock—will shrink even more."

He paid for it.

\* \* \*

By nine, I realized I hadn't eaten all day. It was something that had a tendency to get away from me when I got busy.

I'd been like that when I worked the beat in Brooklyn. It was usually Peter who reminded me to eat. I swear he could have bought stock in Dunkin' Donuts. I closed the shop for half an hour and walked down the street to Sonic. I ordered two bacon double cheeseburgers, large fries, and a monster Mountain Dew to get me through the rest of the night. All that mountain climbing had given me a bit of an appetite, I had to admit. On the way over, I'd given brief thought to dropping into Molly's Steakhouse, but they didn't have takeout, and I didn't think I'd be able to pull that off without looking like a stalker. So I carried my bag of greasy heart attacks down the street, stopped in Dollar General to buy a new pack of peanut M&M's, then headed back to the shop. Things generally slowed down during suppertime, so I doubted I'd missed any customers.

I retrieved the books that Morgana had marked for me and settled on a stool behind the counter, my dinner in one hand and some not-so-light reading in the other while a few customers browsed the shop, looking at mood rings and handmade Shawnee beaded necklaces. None looked particularly enthusiastic, there to kill time until their shift started in one of the many twenty-four hour shops down on the Strip, I knew.

Morgana's book made for interesting reading. The handmade angel dolls were likely effigies used in sympathetic magic, similar to corn poppets in folk magic, or power objects used in Haitian Vodou. The image was representative, but since they were *angels*, I couldn't imagine what they represented aside from actual angels, and the book had nothing to say about that. The idea bothered me. Angels were a uniquely Christian concept not found in those religions. Vodou, mountain conjuring and other pagan religions recognized upper and lower deities. Seldom were they human-shaped or winged.

And there was one other problem with the dolls. In no Christian religion—no religion at all—could a mortal human being hold dominion over an angel. The only thing that could conjure an angel was another angel, so the whole idea was ludicrous.

An old man stepped up to the counter and handed me the third tract of the night. He said in a somber voice, obviously used to being heard, "Young man, have you accepted Jesus Christ as your personal Lord and Savior?"

"I don't think anything can save me, to be honest," I said without looking up from the book.

"You are not beyond salvation. None of us are."

"You might be surprised," I told him, not that he believed me. They never do. If I became a priest and lived in absolute consecrated piety for the rest of my life, I would still die and go to hell. There was no question of that. I knew there was a place set aside just for me.

The front of the tract he'd given me had a picture of badly drawn angels descending a long ladder from Heaven to the earth. Beneath them lay a small suburban house, presumably the house they were protecting from evil things like me. It was then I decided I had to go back to the Berger house and take a look around those woods.

After the old man left, I had one last customer before I was ready to close up shop for the night. A young woman stepped in with bright bottle-red hair. I instinctively looked up, then felt a letdown inside. It wasn't Vivian; it was Holly King. She crept up to the counter like a criminal and said she was interested in books on folk medicine for a school project she was working on, specifically abortifacients.

Le sigh.

# | 6 |

THE FOLLOWING MORNING, I woke to find Ben had left a message on my cell. He said he was going back to interview the Bergers later that morning and I could ride shotgun, if I wanted to. He thought maybe I could glean some kind of information if I went through Cassandra Berger's possessions. Ben labors under the assumption that I can do psychometry, the psychic ability to learn about an object by touching it. It's a nice thought, but I can't do that. I have other mad skills, like the ability to recognize clues. Still, I wasn't about to correct Ben; I wanted to see the Bergers again too much.

I called him back and told him to pick me up on the way. I was fresh from my morning shower and I hadn't overslept. See, I really do know how to act like an adult. After I was dressed and looked human, I put the kettle on in the kitchen. Then I leaned against the sink and called Morgana, who hadn't come home last night. I felt a small stab of guilt when she picked up. She sounded…ahem, busy.

"Yeah, Nick," she said, sounding out of breath and a tad annoyed. Morgana likes early-morning romps, though I can't fathom it myself. I am so not a morning person. Sex in the morning is like breakfast: such things should never happen on this plane of existence.

"Sorry. Interrupting, am I?"

"You are. But you're not sorry about it." I could hear her squirming around in the sheets, probably trying to find a more private position to talk on her cell.

"Is he good?" I asked.

"Nick!"

"Better than me?"

"Nick, stop it. You're such a pervert."

I smiled. "Ben called. He's going back to interview the Bergers again. He wants me along to look at the little girl's room." I paused. "I want to go, Morgana. I want to help find the girl, if I can."

"What do you need from me, Nick?"

"He'll be here around eleven. Any chance you can take the shop then? I don't want to close up with the busy season and all."

I waited while Morgana checked her schedule. "I don't have any appointments until tonight. I'll try to get back by ten."

"I appreciate that."

"You're still a pervert," she said, and hung up.

\* \* \*

Another thing about Ben is he's chronically punctual, and he expects everyone else to be, as well.

At five to ten, I finished gelling my bad haircut into one of those modern spiky men's do's, slid a casual yet cop-like blazer over my pullover, and went downstairs. As the big Swiss-style clock tower standing erect over Blackwater started tolling the tenth hour, Ben pulled up in his police cruiser and I slid into the passenger side, sliding on my favorite pair of rosy sunglasses.

"Looking sharp," Ben said.

"I try to avoid the vagabond look when I talk to suspects. It makes them nervous."

"You really think the Bergers are up to something?" He pulled out onto the main drag and headed west toward the developments. I knew he wouldn't be asking me if this investigation wasn't important to him. But there was the rub: this *was* important to him. So important, he was willing to drag me along. So important, he'd set the kachina doll on his dashboard like it was a bobble-head.

I could imagine Ben putting himself in Thom Berger's place, frantic to find his lost daughter.

"I don't know what the Bergers are up to," I admitted. "I assume you ran a background check?"

"They're clean, Nick. Thom married Rebecca seven years ago. She was a nurse at the time down at Pocono Medical. Graduated from ESU with top grades. Thom's run the True Value since his old man died twenty-five years ago. Not much for education, but it hasn't held him back any. They don't have so much as a parking ticket between them."

"Squeaky clean."

"You say that like it's bad."

I shrugged. "Not bad, just unrealistic."

Ben's squad car smelled greasy, like fast food and donuts. I rolled down the window to let in some fresh air.

"Guilty until proven innocent," Ben said.

"I'm not a cop anymore, Ben. I don't have to play by the rules. I can be as suspicious about people's motives as I like."

"Why'd you quit being a cop?" Ben asked suddenly.

I looked over at his profile. From the front, Ben looked African-American, but from the side I could see his Shawnee roots in the arch of his nose and his high cheekbones. He had a hunter's face. Maybe that's why I liked him. You can trust hunters. They don't have time for deception.

"My partner was killed," I told him. Like he didn't already know that.

"Goes with the territory. A badge is a big ol' target, Nick. You know that."

"I didn't like the way he died. It wasn't normal."

Ben raised his eyebrows at that. "You think it was a hit?"

"I know it was a hit." I really didn't want to talk about this now.

"Was he into some bad shit?" he asked softly. He wasn't using his cop-voice, so I knew this was strictly off the record. "Were you?"

"I was always into bad shit growing up, Ben. But my family is into worse shit."

"Organized crime?"

"Something like that."

Ben didn't ask any more questions, thankfully. Not that I would have answered any more. I'd already told him more than I told most folks. Only Morgana knew the whole story. And after I'd told her everything all those years ago, I could tell she wished she'd never asked.

Five minutes later, we turned up the paved drive to the Berger house and parked next to a bold looking, cherry-red SUV. I recognized the vehicle immediately, and I wasn't the least bit reassured by its appearance. As Ben and I started up the mum-lined walk to the Bergers' front stoop, the door opened and Shelley Preston stepped down onto the stoop. She was talking avidly to Thom Berger about having him on the radio. Somehow, I just wasn't surprised.

I hung back by the SUV as Ben climbed the stoop to talk to Thom Berger. Whatever Shelley had to say to me, it wasn't for Thom Berger or Ben Oswell to hear.

Shelley zeroed right in on me, prancing up in her four-inch pumps, a predatory sway to her hips. Anyone looking on would say she had sex in her walk, but I knew she wanted to eat me alive…and not in a good way. She smiled her professional smile but her eyes were mean and dead. Shark eyes. "Nicky," she cooed, looking me over critically, "it's nice seeing you again so soon. Rockin' that whole retro *Miami Vice* look, I see. How's business?"

I smiled in return. "We're surviving the recession."

"As long as there're superstitious old women living on Social Security, you'll always make out in this town, right?"

*Here we go*, I thought. I lifted my head and smiled. "Wow. This from the woman who sucks the blood of human misery in order to further her career in public radio."

Shelley laughed, a high, light tune that revealed nothing unpleasant. Maybe she was perpetually PMSing, or maybe it was because the Phillies had lost to the Cardinals last night, but she had that whole angry newshound thing going on. Cassandra's disappearance had really brought it out in her. "You ought to write that shit down. You could make a fortune writing fiction."

"You are such a fucking cunt."

She looked at me then with something akin to surprise. "And you're a fucking hypocrite, Englebrecht. Why are you really here?"

I could have fired off about a half dozen things in response, but I held my tongue. When I found that lost camper, I hadn't let the papers report my name. I'd given Ben the credit for that, not because I was feeling particularly humble that day but because my dad had dropped by and warned me not to let my name into the papers. He said it would cause me too much trouble, that I was already attracting unwanted attention. Not long after, Malach had shown up for the first time trying to bust my balls. I hated my dad, but I had to admit he was right most of the time. As a result, Ben was half of the mind that I was dirty and/or on the Tri-State mafia's shit list. Shelley, who had been on the scene when the camper was found, was of the same mind and convinced I had a filthy past I should be ashamed of. Of course, she wanted the details of that filthy past.

That was one-half of the reason why she loved to hate me. The other half was more elemental. After all her hair had fallen out, she'd become convinced that I'd been somehow responsible for that —which, incidentally, I had been.

It was the irony of my life that the one time I turned down a nice piece of ass, it insisted on following me around town, trying to make my life a living hell. But it illustrated a truth I was only recently becoming acquainted with: No good deed goes unpunished.

"I'm here to help the Bergers find their daughter," I told her simply. "Same as you."

"Did Thom Berger hire you?" she asked in full talk-show hostess mode. I'd heard Shelley drill guests into their seats on her show. I knew what she thought, that the whole psychic detective thing was a bullshit front, that I was doing sleazy business in her hometown, she just didn't know what kind yet.

"It was nice talking to you too, Shelley." I started walking away.

"That wasn't much of an answer," she called after me.

I waved her away. "It wasn't much of a question."

Shelley laughed. "You know, it's a damned shame, Englebrecht. The outs

\* \* \*

Amazingly, my day got worse.

Yeah, I know. It surprised me too.

While Ben settled down in the breakfast nook with his notepad, I requested permission from Thom Berger to search Cassandra's room. I didn't really have to—police had been through her room several times—but I thought I would be courteous and ask.

Thom, sitting opposite Ben, looked up at me uneasily. "Everything was already fingerprinted. The cops were through everything yesterday."

"I'm not a cop, Mr. Berger. I'm a clairvoyant. I'd like to see if I can get a psychic imprint of her," I said, which sounded nicely metaphysical, I thought. I had other plans, but the Bergers didn't need to know about any of that.

Thom spread his hands in a way that seemed to state he couldn't stop me. I looked around the kitchen area, searching for Mrs. Berger, but the only one here with us was the Hispanic housekeeper, Zanita, busy preparing tea and coffee. I met her eyes but she quickly looked away, and, I think, crossed herself. That wasn't necessarily an admission of guilt, just good sense.

I went upstairs. The house had that white, shiny, open spaciousness that only new houses have. Even the paint smelled new. I followed a long hallway decorated with a bright Chinese runner. The Bergers' various bedrooms and guestrooms lined the hallway on both sides, but Cassie's room was marked with yellow police tape up ahead.

I ducked under the tape and flipped on the lights.

Nice room. It was done in lavender, instead of the traditional pink, with a poufy canopy bed full of pink and purple stuffed animals. Disney wallpaper arched across the walls in shocking pastel colors, full of various flying creatures like Dumbo and Peter Pan. It was a little too much, the only place Mrs. Berger had gone overboard with the decor, in my humble opinion. At a glance, there was nothing overtly weird or standoutish about the room.

I started at the bed and moved my way clockwise around the room. If it's one thing I know how to do, it's toss a room. When I was a cop, I did vice, not homicide. The two are completely different animals, regardless of what primetime TV will have you believe. I didn't do the stuff you see on *Dexter* and *Hawaii Five-O*. I didn't look at blood splatters or cadavers. I didn't parry with medical examiners or my boss. For eight hours a day, I ripped cold-water flats, motel rooms, and septic project apartments apart, looking for evidence of possession. I got shot at by pimps, pushers, hookers, and kids so high they couldn't aim straight and so young it was enough to make you cry.

I didn't bother to move the mattress. I cut it open using the athame in my boot. By the by, you don't use athames in such manners, but it was sharp and it was what I had at hand. Finding nothing of interest, I went through the bureau and then the hope chest at the foot of the bed where Mrs. Berger kept her daughter's diapers and other care products, looking for false bottoms. I checked the closet, then got down on my knees and started examining the carpet, looking for places where tacks were missing or were newer than the rest—and that was how Zanita found me, on my knees, folding back a piece of beige carpeting in the closet.

I knew the exact moment when she entered the bedroom. I could feel her like a fluttery touch between my shoulder blades. I let the carpet flap down and climbed to my feet, turning. It was pretty appropriate, I thought, me stepping out of the closet. That's where the monsters always come from, right?

"En el nombre del Padre, del Hijo, y del Espíritu Santo. Amén." Zanita crossed herself, then raised her hand and made the sign of the Evil Eye, extending her index and little finger while holding her middle and ringer finger down with her thumb. She said, quite clearly, "Diablo."

I held very still, not wanting to spook the woman. "You are a bruja?"

It took the woman a long moment to answer. "No—but my abuela—my grandmother—she was powerful." She said this like a talisman, no doubt in an effort to summon her grandmother to her side and protect her from the big, bad demon-man.

"I won't hurt you, Zanita," I told her in Spanish. "Your grandmother *was* powerful. She has given you a great gift."

Zanita looked unimpressed. "You will leave this place. You are not welcomed here, devil. You will not hurt the girl."

"You say that like you know the girl is alive."

She watched me carefully, frightened half out of her wits, though I sensed nothing like malice or deception from the woman. Brujos—witches—are generally very easy for me to read. The closer they are to the occult, the closer they are to me, and that makes it very difficult for them to lie to me. Zanita thought me evil, but I could sense great love and concern for little Cassandra. She seemed to weigh her options, ultimately deciding the life of a child was worth speaking to a devil.

"My grandmother came to me and told me the girl is alive. That is all I know."

I took the angel poppet out of my pocket. "Do you know what this is, Zanita?"

Her eyes widened and she made the sign of the cross. "You would curse me, devil?"

"I am not interested in cursing you, Zanita, or this house. I just want to find out what happened to Cassandra." Unfortunately, by the time I had finished speaking, Zanita had turned and fled the room. She said something frantically in Spanish as she made her way down the stairs, nearly tripping over her own feet, and I had a funny feeling she was going to give notice before the day was through.

*Great going, Nick, I thought. Scary much?*

There was a good chance Zanita was going to be talking crazy-like and upsetting the household, so I thought it would help if I hurried up. Before going back downstairs, I ducked into the most well used bedroom I could find, what I thought was Thom and

Rebecca's. I might as well have a glance around before they threw my ass out.

Unlike Cassie's room, Rebecca had outfitted this one with a more localized theme. I saw a Chippendale four-poster bed without a canopy and old-timey prints of vintage cars on the walls. The bed was covered in what was likely a real Amish quilt in a wedding-ring pattern, and there was another quilt in a star pattern hanging on the wall behind a pane of glass. A small plaque stated that Rebecca had won a contest sewing it. There was prescription medication on the bedside table, a cross on the wall, and books on the bookshelves. I went to examine the books and immediately recognized a few as "recipe" books likely written by Thom Berger's own ancestors. His ancestors, like mine, had been deeply into magic and the occult. I was looking over what was likely his ancestor's Book of Shadows when I heard footsteps coming up the stairs.

Rebecca Berger, dressed more conservatively in jeans and a warm pullover, stood in the doorway. Her hair was again in a ponytail. She stared at me shrewdly. "What are you doing in here?"

I looked her over. "You seem a bit more coherent than you were yesterday, Mrs. Berger."

"You don't need to be in here. Get out."

"I'm here to help your daughter."

"I don't need your help, Profane and Wicked Prince."

I stopped and stared at Mrs. Berger carefully. It was entirely possible that she had spoken to Zanita in the last few moments, but I seriously doubted the bruja would have been able to convince her employer that anything as outlandish as me existed in so short a time.

"Well, well, well. The gloves come off." I shrugged my shoulders and tried to "feel" her out, but Rebecca's aura was a blank. That is, she felt human to me. Muffled. It's possible for certain creatures to hide their natures from me, especially if they know who I am.

I'm the son of an archangel, but I'm hardly perfect.

I set the Book of Shadows down on the bed. "Who are you?" I asked in the Divine language, the language of the angels. It was the same language that Malach favored. The one that sounded like you were simultaneously clearing your throat and trying to summon Cthulhu up from R'lyeh. Seriously, I don't know what's divine or angelic about it. It always reminds me of someone speaking German with strep throat.

Rebecca Berger looked at me carefully. "Why should I tell the Prince of Air my name, that he may hold dominion over me?"

"You will tell me your name because it is my birthright to ask."

Rebecca, or the thing *inside* of Rebecca, considered me. I was getting just a little sick of being called fancy Biblical names, but I watched her speak. Just like interviewing suspects, how a demonically controlled person speaks is just as important as what they say. I've seen a lot of demonic possession over the years. The thing that always gets me is how nearly perfect it is. *Nearly* being the important word here. Almost invariably, the person under the influence of possession speaks languages and utilizes syntaxes unknown to them. After all, they're merely a demon's poppet. Its voice-piece. To put it another way, they operate like a badly pirated movie where the visual and audio are working just a hair out of synch.

Rebecca's synch was very good. Her voice was neutral, non-threatening. Absolutely non-demonic, except for the words she used. She'd either been possessed a very long time, or she was faking it. Either way, she *would* speak to me. She *would* answer my questions.

The demonic hosts are under my dominion.

"Tell me who you are," I said. As I spoke, I made eye contact with her and held her even gaze. There were no pyrotechnics involved in the spell, nothing very exciting or dramatic. From the outside, it just looked like a silly staring match between two grown people, but I did reach out and capture her. The creature, whatever it was, was mine for the moment. I could feel it wriggling inside of Rebecca Berger's body like a fish caught out of water. It was a piece of her, but also a piece *apart* from her. If it was of demonic origin, it would be forced to obey me, regardless of its status or age. If it was something else, it would likely break my hold on it very quickly.

"Who are you?" I again demanded. I moved closer to Rebecca and extended my hand as if I might touch her.

When I was almost upon her, she smiled. It was an old, ugly smile. "Beast," she told me. "I *know* you."

"Lovely. Is that supposed to impress me?"

"Man of Sin. Son of Perdition. Your father calls."

"I don't take his calls anymore." Yes, I can be a total asshole to demons. It's even a little bit fun.

"You," she said. "You are the Dragon in the Pit. You are the man who will swallow the moon..."

"That's rather melodramatic, don't you think?"

"He burns."

"Who burns?" I said.

"Peter. He burns."

I felt my stomach lurch at the words. The thing inside Rebecca moved, slithering around like a wet snake. I knew it was full of lies. I knew it would try to deceive me. Still, that realization didn't make things any easier. I calmed myself, though I felt my hands shaking. I clenched them both into tight fists. They felt hot. "You lie."

"I know."

"You know nothing. You deceive."

"He burns, Nicky. He lives on in the bottomless pit."

"No," I said. "He doesn't. He was a good man."

"He cries, Nicky. He cries in hell. Who has put him there?"

"You're nothing but a lying cunt of a demon."

"You don't eat right, Nick," Rebecca Berger said in Peter's voice.

I stopped only a few paces away from Rebecca as the world swirled around me in a surreal spectacle of light and colors. That was something that Peter had said to me on the last day of his life. Those were the words he'd spoken in the car the morning before he'd died. We'd stopped for coffee and donuts and I'd bitched about how clichéd it all was. Then Peter laughed and invited me downtown to his mom's for dinner that night. She was making eggplant parmesan. She had been heating it in the oven when I arrived to tell her about Peter.

I looked deep into the depths of Rebecca's eyes and saw only more depths. "They fuck him, Nicky," she said sweetly, smiling. She blinked, and the thing inside of her moved again. "The demons fuck him, Nicky, every day, all day. And he *screams* for you..."

I felt a rush of heat all through my body. I hadn't realized I'd moved. Suddenly I was standing over Rebecca, my arms raised as if to strike her. Rebecca was on the floor at my feet, cowering, her arms over her head, rocking violently back and forth and screaming in a way that made every hair on my body stand at rigid attention.

Everything happened fast after that. Within seconds, I heard footsteps thumping on the carpeted stairs, and I could see Thom Berger's bald palate rising up past the spindles of the banister as he raced toward us. He was shouting for his wife while Rebecca screamed on and on, hysterically, like a machine with no end.

I instinctively backed away as first Thom, then Ben, burst through the doorway of the bedroom. I backed until I hit the wall, the cross, and then jerked reflexively away before it could burn its way into my back. Everyone's attention settled on Rebecca, then on me as if I had done something to her, something hideous and depraved.

Ben immediately moved between me and Rebecca like a referee. Thom rushed to Rebecca's side on the floor and gathered her into his arms. She began to writhe, then scream again, her entire body electric with terror. He hushed her. She looked up. She saw me. She screamed louder still and clawed at his back.

Thom turned to Ben, his face contorted with an almost inhuman rage and shouted, "Get him out of here!"

Ben swiveled on his heels and I felt his hand latch onto my arm like a snake biting down. His face was pallid. I had never seen a black man so pale in all my life. "Get *out*, Nick. *Now*." His voice wasn't angry, not yet, but the timber was deep and resonating. He showed his gleaming white teeth like a dog about to bite. "Back to the cruiser."

I knew I was done. Just like I knew Ben wasn't going to require my services here any longer. I yanked my arm loose and stomped from the room while Rebecca Berger writhed in her husband's arms and screamed hysterically about her lost Cassie and how the Devil had taken her away.

Devil, indeed.

# | 7 |

I SPENT THE latter part of the day and the early part of the evening down at the Blackwater Police Department. They put me in their very small interrogation room with a cooling cup of untouched coffee and left me sitting there for over two hours. The building is small, about the size of a double-wide trailer. It sort of looks like one too. Besides Ben, there's one chief deputy, two DAs that serve the whole county, and four deputies. The interrogation room doesn't have fancy two-way mirrors or insulated walls. It has a folding table and two folding chairs. Blackwater isn't exactly gangland Chicago. I could hear the officers talking sports and joking just outside. I was told not to move until Ben got back. I wasn't sure what they would do to me if I tried to leave. Revoke my library card, maybe.

Ben banged in at about a quarter to six. I expected angry. I got livid.

"Nick, what the fuck?" he yelled at me. The activity in the other room immediately went on hiatus. You could have heard the proverbial pin drop. Then Ben seemed to catch himself, snorted a deep breath through his nose, and said in a lower voice, "I could cite your ass right *now*."

I leaned on the table and said, "For what? I never touched her, Ben."

"Thom Berger called the chief to complain. He wants to sue the department. He said you wanted to hit his wife."

"I did *not* hit his wife," I said as evenly as possible. "I'm sure he took her to Emergency. They'll confirm I never laid a hand on her."

He pointed a savage finger at me. "You made me look like an ass, Nick!" He stomped around the room while he got his temper back under control. I waited patiently. Then he asked, "What did you say to her to make her go off like that?"

"Nothing." I felt a twinge. Lying to the police wasn't something that sat well with me. That was called Obstruction of Justice. It was also called being a shitty cop. "I didn't say anything."

"You accused her of doing away with her own kid, didn't you?"

"No." Not a lie.

"What were you doing in the Bergers' bedroom?"

"Looking for clues."

"You were supposed to be looking through the girl's bedroom, doing your hoodoo. You're not a cop, Nick. What the hell's the matter with you?"

"She did it."

Ben stopped ranting and stomping and looked at me. "Did she confess to something?

"No. But I know she did it. She's not insane. She's faking."

Ben leaned over the folding table, gritting his teeth. "The paramedics said she may have suffered a stroke, Nick. You don't fake a stroke."

"She may have suffered a stroke because her body was under extreme duress."

"What's that supposed to mean?"

"I think Rebecca Berger is possessed."

Ben glared at me. For one moment, Ben almost looked like he wanted to believe me. It was like a miniature war going on between his practical and spiritual sides. In the end, his practical side won out. "You're done here, Nick. Get the fuck out. And if I see you anywhere *near* the Bergers, I will put your ass in jail personally."

\* \* \*

"The prodigal son returns," Morgana said when I finally stepped into the shop at nightfall. She was selling a pair of college kids some books on magic. "I thought you'd never get back."

"Well, as you can see, I'm back."

Morgana stared at me a long, hard moment. "You are. Could you take the shop until closing? Anton is coming by to pick me up tonight. I'm speaking to his coven about crystal magic."

I slid my arms out of my blazer and crumpled it up. Strangely, I felt sore all over, like I'd taken some knocks in a bar fight or something. And tired. I did not want to watch the shop until closing. Unfortunately, I had no choice. One of the college girls started checking me out, being pretty obvious about it. I glared at her until she looked away.

"Are you all right?" Morgana asked me after the college bunnies had left the store.

I smiled, emptily. "Peachy," I answered, assuming my place behind the counter.

\* \* \*

At a quarter to eleven, Vivian stepped into the shop. I looked up from the Chinese menu I was perusing, not very enthusiastically, and spotted her standing by the door. She was wearing a long, untucked chambray shirt and a short tartan skirt, black stockings and penny loafers. She looked childish and vulnerable, and the moment I spotted her, my whole world shrank down to just Vivian.

My heart quickened and I became aware of a gnawing ache in the vicinity of my groin. It had been a rotten day and I had a ridiculous notion. I wanted to go to her and steal her away. I wanted to hold her against me until I was warm and comforted again. I wanted her beneath me, writhing ecstatically on my sheets.

I had thought that the days of separation had built up a false fantasy of Vivian. Her skin could not be so white and flawless, her hair so rose red. Her eyes were not at all like aquamarines. Yet when I saw her, I knew my memory of her was sharp and clear and focused. I knew all these things were real. It was all I could do to keep from trembling at the sight of her.

"Vivian?" I said, coming out from behind the counter. "Is everything all right?"

She shook her head. Her eyes were filling with fearful tears. "Nick, it's Malach."

\* \* \*

I closed the shop up early and escorted Vivian upstairs. She started to shake then, and I led her to the sofa so she could sit down. She sat on the end of the cushion and said, "He's been following me, Nick. I only just got away tonight because I remembered what you said. There was a Jehovah's Witness hall nearby. I ducked under the eaves and just sat in the entranceway until he got tired and went away. I didn't even know if it would work. He had a gun..." She looked at me directly then. She looked so young. "What does he want with me?"

I told her the truth. "I think he wants to kill you."

She stared down at the floor between her feet. "What can I do to stop him?"

I brushed a few strands of her hair off her face. The touch of her skin was electric to me. "You can fight him, or you can run away from him. Right now, I would suggest running, until you learn to fight. Until you're strong. If you can find a holy place to live, it will help. Even Malach can't spill blood on holy ground."

"Like a monastery?"

"Any holy place will do. Even one that's been deconsecrated at some point. A church that's been renovated into apartments, for instance. Something like that." I closed my eyes as her fear and power seeped into me. Just being this close made me ache to hold her, to be inside of her. "Let me make some tea. Then we'll talk about it."

I got up and moved to the kitchen area. I started filling the kettle, keeping my back to Vivian, but before it was even half-full, I sensed her closing in. I shut the tap off and turned to find her standing there, staring up at me in that girlish way she had. I don't even think she knew what she was doing to me. She was a daemon. Her power was elemental and sexual. You cannot get more basic than sexual power. It is the root of every living thing.

Vivian said, her voice trembling, "Ever since that night, the night we met, I've been thinking about you, Nick." She frowned and stared down at her raggedly chewed fingernails. "I dream about you constantly. I daydream about you at work. I can't seem to think straight anymore. What's happening to me?" She looked ashamed, disconcerted.

I leaned against the counter and said, "It's because you're like me."

"A daemon."

"Yes."

"Are there many? Of us, I mean."

"I really don't know," I told her. "You're the first I've encountered in a decade. No, I don't think there are many."

She looked up at me from beneath her furrowed brows. "Are we...normal?"

"In what way?"

"I mean…are we like humans? Do we function like human beings?"

"Yes and no. Mostly yes."

"We don't do anything weird?"

"Such as?"

"I don't know. Shapeshift. Drink blood."

I smirked at her sincerity. "No. Not to my knowledge. Except on the full moon."

She looked horrified.

"I'm joking," I said.

She let her breath out in relief. "So I could live normally? I could have a family?"

"I really don't know, Vivian," I said in all honesty. I had no idea if we were "normal" in any biological sense. I slept. I ate. I had never been sick, but that might have just been me, not me being a daemon. I could be injured on both a physical and spiritual level, but I had never fathered a child, though there had been ample opportunities for that. Perhaps we daemons could not. There was no one for me to ask these questions of. I had been on my own since I was four years old. I had had to learn everything the hard way.

Vivian took a deep breath and let it out, like she'd come to a momentous decision. "Could we be together tonight?" she asked, then paused. She looked up at me curiously, nervously. She was terrified, I realized, terrified I would send her away. And so horny she couldn't hold still. "I've never been with another daemon…one of my own…species."

I smiled at that. I thought of some prosaic things to say. Instead, what came out of my mouth was, "I've wanted you since the first day I saw you, Vivian. So yes, we can be together. If it's what you want."

She brightened considerably. She leaned into me and I captured her face. I stroked my thumbs along her cheeks. I leaned down—I was too tall and she too short—and slanted my mouth against hers. I'd meant it to be a soft, exploratory kiss. The first kiss. I'd wanted to be gentle with her. I didn't want to spook her. Yet the moment I tasted all that soft wetness inside her mouth, her body responded like it had been made only for me. She gripped me at the hips and jerked me against her. Her aggression both surprised and thrilled me. I cupped the back of her head to hold her in place while I slid my tongue deep inside her mouth. I kissed her hard, a bruising kiss. I fucked her mouth with my tongue. I slid my hands up her sides, under her arms, and finally palmed the soft mounds of her breasts through the thin shirt. I wondered if I was going too fast, frightening her, but she gripped my ass, urging me on.

I tried to stop kissing her, to ask her if this was really what she wanted. She couldn't be more than twenty years old, a child really. I was forty-four. The situation was ridiculous and inappropriate. Still, she kept her hands where they were, holding me in place so she could kiss and taste me.

"Viv..." I began, but she hushed me, kissed me silent. Her kiss was both tender and demanding, and her mouth tasted like cinnamon, fire.

She was delicious, all I wanted, everything I had been waiting for. I moved my mouth to her throat and she tilted her head back for me, a long white column against a wash of burning crimson hair. I loved her then, I think. The way she trusted me enough to give me her throat. I worked my way down to the top button of her shirt. Again, I stopped, waiting with my heart thudding in my throat to see if she would protest while the ache inside of me turned into an angry, primal pain.

For the first time in my life—the only time—I had to make a concentrated effort not to force myself upon another human being.

If she turned me away now, I wasn't sure what would happen. I didn't even want to consider it.

She must have known. She must have felt it. She brought her hand to the front of my body and touched me through my jeans. I groaned and bit the side of her pretty neck. Not a hard bite—I did not even break the surface of her skin—but she whimpered all the same. She tightened her hold on me, controlling my desire, and I growled against her throat and thrust against her involuntarily like some animal in heat. She turned her head and said in the shivery cup of my ear, "I want you, Nick. Tonight. I want you to fuck me."

"I'd rather love you."

"First fuck me, then love me."

Her eyes looked different when I pulled away. Wilder. Older. They were daemon eyes, which are different from human eyes. Daemon eyes see things that human beings cannot. They see beyond the Veil, beyond the edges of the universe. They see the Old Gods, the ones that came before the One God. They look different as a consequence.

I undid Vivian's blouse, trying not to tear it from her body in my haste. Under the shirt, she wore an exquisite black lace bra that made her skin glow like pearl. Something about the contrast of the black lace underwear under all that conservative, studious clothing made me want her even more. It made me want to hold her and protect her and possess her. I told her how beautiful and fuckable she was as I worked first on the shirt and then on the bra. I told her other things, perverse things, things you don't say to your girlfriend or wife. I talked to her like some common gutter slut, like some fuckthing, but the more I talked, the more excited she became.

I'd managed to undo the front closure of the bra. Her nipples were pierced through with tiny silver barbells. I lowered my head to her breast and took one in my mouth, hard, like I meant to hurt her. She grunted and sank her fingernails into my hair, but the angle was all wrong for this kind of pleasure making. I turned and lifted her so she was sitting on the counter in front of me. That put us closer to eye level.

She said things to me then to encourage me, filthy things that nice girls don't say. Her eyes shone savagely. She wrangled the pullover off me and ran her fingertips over my ribs. Her nails left angry red marks behind. I shivered and ducked my head so I could turn my greedy affections back to her pretty, swollen nipples. I wondered if the piercings hurt. I bit and suckled them until she gasped for breath and opened her legs to me. She gripped my ass, and dragged me against her until my knees hit the front of the cupboards. I groaned at the pressure of my erection under her belly, at the way she commanded me, demanded of me, controlled me.

I had never met a girl like Vivian before. She had the most beautiful filthy mouth, the most vicious claws. "Nick," she hissed in my ear as she undid my jeans, none too gently. "Now, Nick, *now*."

Under her skirt, her bikini underwear was black lace like the bra. I hooked it with my fingers and slid it down just far enough for me to find my way inside her. The first hard thrust caught Vivian unawares. She arched her back and screamed from the pain of the impact. She was tight and I was big, especially at that moment. My father's gift to me. The angels have no genitalia at all, but the higher demons are hung like horses. She was wet, but I had given her no warning. Anyway, there was no way for someone to prepare themselves for that. I stopped, locked deep inside of her, unable to move, and waited to see if she would reject me, if she would fight me.

Vivian squirmed and grunted and sweated through the pain, trying to acclimate herself to my size. I put a hand between us. There was some blood. She wasn't a human virgin, I'm sure, but she had been a daemon virgin until that moment. Her mouth worked for a moment, and then she finally said, "Jesus, Nick."

"Do you want me to stop?"

Vivian looked at me with feral catlike eyes. "No. I want you to fuck me, Nick. I want you to fuck me hard."

I fucked her hard. It wasn't lovemaking. It wasn't even sex. Human beings engage in sex. Animals have a rut. I rutted with Vivian, and all that Brownswick had said in the woods came back to me in that moment. Each impact pushed her shoulders back against the cupboards. Each made her grunt as I opened her up a little more. Things would get better. They would even be good. For now, though, there was going to be some pain and blood. I shuddered in the last moments, my face buried in her hair, trying to hold and comfort her even as I hurt her. She felt so warm inside, and her skin was almost feverish to the touch. She whimpered as she came with me, against me, devouring me.

When it was over, I withdrew from her, trying not to cause her additional harm. Vivian groaned, and her hands clutched my shoulders in a death grip. She shivered violently at every lurching move. She was tender inside, I knew, and would be for hours to come. She might even come to hate me.

I waited.

Vivian pressed her smile into my throat. "Thank you, Nick," she told me. "*Now* you can love me."

# | 8 |

AFTER WE GOT into bed, I lay there holding Vivian until she was ready again. Then I let her have her way with me. It seemed only fair.

She liked being on top, I learned, and she liked controlling my rhythm. I didn't mind being her wingman. It was a nice change from the women I'd known in the past, the ones who needed everything but a damned manual to follow along. Afterward, she touched me all over and asked me if female daemons were different from human women in some way. I told her I didn't really know. That led to questions about daemon anatomy, which led to questions about my parentage. I'd planned to put off telling her about my mom and dad until I knew she wanted a relationship with me, but she was curious, as any person might be. I felt I owed her that, at least.

"My mom was born right here in Blackwater," I told her, holding her against me. "Her name was Wilhelmina Wodehouse."

Vivian knew the Wodehouse name. They had been living here in Blackwater as long as the Kings and Rinkleys—a point of contention with those families, I knew. I told her the Wodehouses were one of the founding families who came over on the Mayflower, and that my mother's family had always had a weird history. Both the Wodehouses and Bergers had been regarded as witches and conjurers and were barely tolerated by the Plymouth colony. That had encouraged them to migrate farther west and settle here while witches and normal women were being hanged en masse in Salem. It had probably saved my bloodline from extinction.

"And your father?" she asked. She lay clasping me, one hand brushing over the blond hairs of my chest.

I hesitated then. There was no easy way to explain this, so I just told her. I told her everything I knew about *him*. Then I waited. I could hear the blood washing in my ears. I could feel my heartbeat and hers. I wondered if she would run screaming into the night as any sensible human being would do. But she surprised me.

"Have you...met your father?" She said it softly as if afraid she might conjure something malevolent out of the dark if she spoke too loudly.

"He's visited me a few times. But we don't get along."

"Your mother...did she know?"

"No. He seduced her young and married her. He used the name Englebrecht. I suppose it was a joke to him. Englebrecht means 'angel-breaker' in German."

Vivian waited, so I forced myself on. "He stayed with her until she was impregnated with me, then he disappeared. The pregnancy was so unusual that my mother began to research it, and him. She sought mediums and psychics, and there were a good many witches in her own family, as you can imagine. When she finally learned who—and what—he was, she put all kinds of wards around the house to keep him out. She was so afraid my father would return to take me away from her."

She looked uncomfortable. "Did he?"

"He returned several times, but I don't recall those times clearly. My mother later told me she would look out a window and see him playing with me in the backyard, pushing me on the swings, that type of thing. After a while, she was so afraid she took us to New

York, to stay with her sister there. My mother hoped that the anonymity of the city would help hide us, but he found us. I supposed you can't hide from the Devil."

I thought about that day, the day my life changed, though so much of it was a blur to my child's mind. "I was four years old when he came calling. He was livid that we had tried to run away from him. He broke all the wards like they were nothing. That was the day he took my mother away. I never saw her again."

I paused. "You see, it was she he wanted all along, not me."

Vivian watched me carefully. "Is your mother dead?"

"I don't know. I don't think so. I think he just took her, to keep her with him."

"But not you."

"No," I answered, perhaps bitterly. "Not me."

I was a selfish person, I knew. I hated my father, not because he was the Father of All Evil, but because of what he had done to my family. "He let me grow up alone. My aunt tried to raise me, she did the best she could, but she had a weak heart and she died very young. After that, I sort of drifted through foster care until I was eighteen. By then, I'd been in trouble with the law so many times you could have wrapped your next birthday gift in my rap sheet. I knew all the cops who worked the precinct by name."

She smiled then, but only a little.

"One of the cops suggested I join the force. He said that way I could spend the same amount of time downtown and be paid for it. So I joined the Police Academy."

She rested her head on my shoulder. She ran her fingertips lightly over my chest. "Why didn't you stay in New York? Why come back here?"

I thought about telling her the rest, but I wasn't ready to talk about Peter. Not yet. I wasn't ready to talk about that night, though I remembered it vividly. I never had such a strong memory before, or since. The leering way the shadows looked, the sour smell of the place where Peter had died.

Peter and I had been doing a routine search for possession in a project in downtown Brooklyn. He went downstairs and I went up. It was our usual pattern—but then something happened. Peter didn't respond to his radio. I knew something was wrong long before I sensed any danger. I knew Peter had been overcome. I just didn't understand why I hadn't heard any struggles or gunshots, the usual indicators.

I rushed to the basement. It was there that I found them, the group of occultists. They were holding some kind of ceremony and Peter had either interrupted it or they had been waiting for him. I never really learned the truth. They had bound and gagged Peter. Their butchery had been fast and efficient, almost surgical, maybe even painless. I don't know. I don't want to know. In the short ten minutes we'd been separated, the occultists had removed all of Peter's reproductive organs, his liver, and his kidneys. They had divided those organs into pieces for their ceremony and had begun ritually consuming them. They were working on his stomach and intestines, working their way up his body, when I found them.

They immediately scattered but I chose not to pursue them. I stayed with Peter instead and called the paramedics. He was still alive when they arrived, though he died en route to the hospital of his wounds. I never learned the truth of why it had happened, or what the people in the basement were trying to do, though I knew my father was behind it somehow. He had to be. Maybe it was a test and I had failed. Maybe it was just plain malice. I just don't know.

"I just wanted to return home, I guess," I told Vivian. That sounded sensible and normal. "And by then, I was very good friends with Morgana. We'd talked about opening an occult shop together."

Naturally, Vivian wanted to know who Morgana was. Or rather, who she was to me.

I told her. "My spiritual adviser. My friend. And a damned good witch. Though we met by accident. I busted her for possession down in New York. Morgana is a very good herbalist, though she sometimes requires a little something...illegal." I showed her the case of opium cigarettes I keep in my tableside drawer. "Morgana makes them. They're excellent for visions."

"You are very bad," she said with a smile. She wanted to try one, so I lit it for her. She leaned against me and closed her eyes as she chased the dragon, and I learned that Vivian was a very frustrated ex-smoker.

"Don't bother torturing yourself," I told her. "The cigarettes won't kill you, believe me. I've been chain-smoking since I was nine years old and there's absolutely nothing wrong with my physiology. I stopped going for checkups in my mid-thirties. The doctors were starting to get suspicious. They were afraid I might be an alien or something. I couldn't bring myself to explain to them that I was a Lucifer." I took the cigarette from her, sucked in the soothing cold smoke, and blew it out my nose. Then I gave it back to her.

"I don't understand," she said.

"My father told me, not very long ago, that there is not one Lucifer, but several. Like a royal bloodline. The original was my grandfather. My father inherited the position from him in the twelfth century and has held the position for about eight hundred years now. Each of the Lucifers is a Man of Sin, but each has a sin that is unique to him, a signature sin, so to speak. My grandfather's sin was vanity and pride, and because of it, there has been enormous dissidence and disobedience to God on Earth. My father's sin is war. He has generated slaughter and pestilence for nearly a thousand years."

She looked at me seriously, her eyes wide. "What's your sin?"

"I don't know. That's for me to discover. Cigarettes, maybe."

She didn't laugh. She wriggled around a little before settling against me, her head on my shoulder. I could tell that she trusted me, despite all the crazy shit I was heaping upon her. "What happens when you discover your sin, Nick?"

It took me a moment to answer. "I...Ascend. Or Descend, depending on how you look at things. It means I get an all expenses paid trip to hell."

She turned and leaned over me, placing her hands on my chest. "You become the Devil."

I watched her carefully. She believed me. I realized that. I also realized she was probably scared out of her mind.

"Do you want to leave now?" I asked. "I'll drive you home, if you want. I know none of this is normal..." I reached up and gathered her hair in my hand. It was soft and almost fey. She was such a pretty girl. Perhaps I had revealed too much. She couldn't want to stay with me. It wasn't normal, but if she left, I felt like I would die inside. Ridiculous, but true.

Slowly she shook her head. "I'm not afraid of you, Nick." She leaned down and kissed me. It was a gentle kiss compared to the violence we had shared earlier. "I'm not normal either," she said as she climbed on top of me. She leaned down, her long red hair tenting us in together, and kissed my mouth and chin and throat. Her piercings rubbed deliciously against my chest. It made me groan. I slid my hands around her ribs and jerked her against me.

Of course I was hard again. It goes without saying. I had this magnificently beautiful and perverted redhead sitting on me. It was impossible not to be. She found me and stroked me. I tried to draw her down upon my erection but she held herself apart.

"Could I be a witch?" she asked, her eyes glimmering. "Could I be strong like you?"

I smiled at that. I wasn't feeling very strong at the moment. Quite the opposite.

"Could you teach me, Nick?"

"What do you want to learn?"

She thought about that as she stroked me softly. She could be incredibly tender when she wanted to be. "What kind of things do you think I'd be good at?"

I said it before I even thought about it. "Sex magic."

"Could you teach me sex magic?"

I rolled her over and pinned her to the mattress. I buried my face in her hair. I told her to lie still and to think only of me. She said that would be no problem at all. She clutched my shoulders with her blood red nails as I took her, slowly at first, then thrusting deep inside her wetness, deeper than anyone had ever gone before. I thrust until she groaned and wrapped her legs around my waist. I imagined our flesh as shining white liquid merging together into one body, into one flesh. I sought that power within myself, that power that was my father and my mother combined—my father the demon, my mother the witch. I imagined it all shining, burning white light, as hot and holy as flames. I opened myself up to it and let Vivian see what a daemon's power looked like.

Vivian groaned, and her head fell back on the pillow. Her eyes widened at the realization that I could share such raw power with her—that I was willing to. Her nails pierced my back. And like the natural witch and daemon she was, she began to feed on that power.

* * *

Waking alone the following morning, I immediately discovered two things. 1. My pack of Camels was missing, and 2. There was someone rattling around my kitchen. I climbed naked out of bed, took the Tanaka from the second drawer of my bedside table, checked the munitions, and stepped into the kitchen, ready to take a bead on someone if necessary.

I had charms and wards secreted away in various places around the loft to prevent invasion by other-creatures—but charms don't keep out human beings. Hey, I might be a witch, but I'm no hippie navel-gazer. And Blackwater might not be New York City, but it wasn't the Garden of Eden, either. If someone gave me due cause, I'd blow their brains out the back of their head. I needed to repaint this place anyway.

I let out my breath when I saw it was Vivian. She was naked and dressed only in a white chef's apron, the one from the kitchen drawer at the bottom that I never use because I can't cook for shit. She was standing at the counter where we'd made love last night—or rather, fucked each other's brains out. She was mixing together some witchy concoction of eggs and milk with a whisk, the back of the open apron framing her absolutely devastating, heart-shaped ass. It was the kind of ass women envy and men dream about. Constantly.

I leaned in the open doorway and used the muzzle of the Tanaka to rub at my beard as I admired the view. She turned and stared at me. She looked me up and down. Then she arched an eyebrow. "Nice gun."

"Thanks." I smiled.

"You're such a cliché, Nick. Do you want some breakfast?"

"Food in the morning is gross. Where're my cigarettes?" I said in my best early-morning bear voice.

She gave me a stern look, unimpressed by my blustering. She walked over to hand me my pack of Camels. She had smoked most of them down, not that I minded. I minded more that she was trying to feed me breakfast, which is absolutely fucking disgusting. "Go wash up and put your gun away, grumpy. Breakfast will be ready in half an hour."

Twenty minutes later, I'd dragged myself back to the kitchen. I'd showered and dressed and shaved. I was ready to eat breakfast.

Since I *never* ate breakfast, I decided this was a good indication that I was utterly and completely in love with Vivian.

She was impressed with my clean-cut appearance and said as much. My father is the most beautiful of all angels. Like David Bowie, only better. Neil Gaiman got that right, at least. I look like my dad. That's advantageous because I look like shit in the morning but no one ever complains. I dropped into a chair at Aunt Lydia's kitchen table and smoked and watched Vivian slide a glass Pyrex dish into the wall oven.

"I baked French toast. It's made with cinnamon, cloves, and nutmeg." Vivian explained like she was teaching a cooking class. She bent over to check the temperature on the oven and I learned a deep appreciation for cinnamon, cloves, and nutmeg in that moment. "Unlike traditional French toast, it's made in the oven. I won a competition for it at school last year."

After she was satisfied the French toast was well on its way, she climbed into my lap and ringed her arms around my neck. I loved the way she felt there, the press of her breasts and sharp little nipples into my chest, even through the apron. I liked the apron a lot more on her than on me. She was wet as she kissed me good morning. I could feel it through my jeans, not that I minded. She took the cigarette from my mouth and frenched it long and hard. "We have to wait twenty minutes," she told me. "But I guarantee it's worth it. You'll love eating my French toast, Nick."

"I'm sure I will," I told her.

# | 9 |

MORGANA GOT BACK from Anton's around eleven o'clock. She had left a message on my cell, probably telling me she'd be back by then to open the shop, but I hadn't checked any of my messages. I was bad with cell phones. Also, I'd been preoccupied.

Vivian was lying on the kitchen table, her hair half in our sticky plates of maple syrup, my face buried in her muff, when Morgana walked into the kitchen. I noticed. Vivian did not. She was too busy enjoying the effects of our sex magic. We had learned quite a few things about her power that morning, including the fact that Vivian's sexual energy was incredibly potent. She could even heal herself through it. I had never met anyone, human or otherwise, who could heal injuries through sex. And yet, she wasn't a succubus. A succubus can only draw power through her partner's body, usually by killing him. Vivian did not need to drain power, and she did not need to kill. She had it all inside herself already. The sex only released it.

Morgana turned and stalked out of the kitchen. Uh-oh, spaghetti-os.

I stopped and eased Vivian up. "I think it would be best if you got dressed now," I told her softly.

Vivian looked at me uncertainly. "Is something wrong?"

"No," I lied. "After you get dressed I'd like you to go downstairs to the shop and gather together the things I told you about."

"All right."

After she'd left the kitchen, I started cleaning up the mess we'd made. Then it occurred to me that Vivian was headed for the bedroom where we'd left her clothes. That meant she and Morgana were likely going to have a few minutes of quality girl time alone. I dropped the plates clattering in the sink, wiped my hands on a kitchen towel, and headed for the bedroom myself.

Things weren't *too* ugly when I arrived. Morgana stood leaning against the closet, listening to Vivian explain about what we'd discovered about her power. Vivian sat on the bed, one leg curled up under her, dressed in her black bikini underwear. I stopped in the doorway and Morgana looked over at me with an absolutely blank expression. "Vivian was explaining about the sex magic."

Vivian looked at me, then at Morgana, then at me. She seemed to sense the tension in the air because she dressed faster than anyone I'd ever seen. In less than two minutes, she was standing in front me exactly as I had seen her the night before.

"I'll be downstairs, Nick," she said, lowered her head, and hurried from the room.

To her credit, Morgana waited until the apartment door had closed before she ripped into me. "What is she doing here?" Her voice dripped ice.

Normally, I would never have tolerated anyone talking to me like that, but I had broken the house rules, and now I had to pay. We had an understanding between us that neither of us would bring our conquests home. The apartment was something we shared. Neutral ground, both physically and spiritually.

I leaned into the doorway and hooked my fingers in my jeans belt loops. "I didn't bring her home. She came here on her own."

"And you let her stay?"

"Morgana, she's a daemon and Malach was after her. What was I supposed to do, throw her out onto the street to be slaughtered?"

She eyed me levelly. "That's awfully dramatic, don't you think, Nick? You could have phoned one of the safe houses. There are a dozen covens in this area alone that would have taken her in."

"Vivian needed help. I was there to help her."

"By teaching her sex magic."

"She wants to be a witch. And I'd like you to teach her."

"No."

I blinked. "Excuse me?"

"I said no. I will not teach that…Vivian magic."

I knew what she had meant to say. She had meant to call Vivian a *thing*. The sudden spurt of rage made my hands clench. My entire body stiffened at the realization. "You don't want to teach Vivian because she's a daemon," I said, trying to keep my voice from growling.

Morgana looked at me carefully, as if I might fly at her. "I don't want to teach her, Nick, because she's evil."

I laughed then, hoarsely. "Don't you think that is just slightly ridiculous to say to *me*?"

She shook her head. "You're not evil, Nick. At least, not yet. But Vivian is. I can sense it."

"You can sense she's an evil person."

She closed her eyes as she thought. I knew she was reading the ambient vibes that Vivian had left behind. "I sense evil within her. A powerful evil. If she learns magic, she may also learn a way to unleash that evil." She opened her eyes. "You're only acting this way because she's a daemon and you want her."

"I do want her. She *is* a daemon. But I also want to protect her."

"Birds of a feather, right?"

"What's that supposed to mean?" I was shouting now and I didn't care. I had never seen Morgana so resistant.

She looked at me steadily, staring me down as always. She was the only person I had ever met who was truly unafraid of me. "You demons are all alike. In the end, it's all in the family, isn't it? You always look after your own."

I never thought about what I was doing. I stomped forward and took Morgana's delicate throat in my hand. I lifted her up so her back scraped against the closet door and we were eye to eye.

"I am not a demon!" I spat, which was pretty absurd, considering our present situation.

Morgana began to gag. Then she clutched my arm. She touched me, and the cold fire of her touch raced up my arm and into my body. The power was sickening, overwhelming. I knew she was calling on her human familiar for protection, a seven-year-old girl named Emily who died violently in a fire almost three hundred years ago. Emily is a spirit guide, powerful and pure. A virgin and a Christian. She's everything I'm not, and she hates me. She's warned me on several occasions to stay away from Morgana, not that I necessarily listen to the denizens of the afterlife. I also run with scissors and I don't always play well with others.

I dropped Morgana and staggered back. My arm felt frozen where she had touched me.

Morgana landed lightly on her feet as if she had no weight at all. Her eyes looked darker, crazier, holier—more like Emily's than her own. I could see the vague outline of Emily's body contained within Morgana's, like a trick of photography.

"Satan, get thee down," she said in Emily's sweet, lilting soprano voice. She raised her hand to me, bringing her two middle fingers sharply down in an archaic expression of exorcism.

I couldn't be exorcised—I was neither dead, nor truly a demon—but it still managed to hurt like hell. It felt like someone had taken lead weights, attached them to massive fishhooks, and embedded those hooks in my flesh. Before I could even say anything, or apologize, I was down on my hands and knees on the floor, my head bowed, shoulders straining, teeth grinding in agony. I stared at Aunt Lydia's worn green carpeting, breathing roughly through my nose and mouth. Moving was useless. My hands might as well be nailed to the floor. Anyway, it only hurt more if I struggled.

"Tell that cunt to back off!" I shouted at Morgana.

I waited, shoulders tensed. I sensed the exact moment Morgana lowered her hand. I sensed Emily taking her leave from the room. Emily feels like a cold, cutting winter wind, the kind that can kill on contact.

Slowly—very slowly—I climbed to my feet.

"Don't *ever* do that to me again, Nick," Morgana warned, rubbing her throat. Her eyes had lightened to their usual bright wintery grey color. "And do not ask me to teach Vivian magic. I will not."

"Fine," I told her before leaving the room. "I'll teach her myself."

\* \* \*

"Is everything all right?" Vivian asked me as I climbed into the car beside her.

I lit a cigarette. It helped calm me somewhat. "Everything's fine," I lied.

We sat in the delivery alleyway behind the shop. The road here was narrow and still dim, even at this hour of the morning. Next door, Mr. Fernstermacher, who ran the antique shop, was dragging his empty trash cans back in. It occurred to me that I had forgotten trash day. Another reason Morgana was likely to lay into me when I got back to the shop.

I was feeling especially peevish. There's something about being called down by some dead, seven-year-old bitch that's very bruising to the ego. I hated Emily even more than I hated Shelley Preston. At least, with Shelley, I knew where I stood. I knew she was a deceptive bitch who would rip my balls off, given the chance. Emily was an enigma. If she'd been alive today, she'd have been the type of girl who played with My Little Pony at age eighteen instead of screwing a long string of boyfriends like a normal teenage girl. The fact that *that* gave her power over me pissed me off to no end.

It also made me worry. I've noticed over the years that those who wield innocence and piety seemed to be gaining a stronger hold over me. I figured that was probably a bad sign, but I was frankly at a loss as to what to do about it. The one time I mentioned it to Morgana, she suggested I turn to a god—any god—for an answer. She thought it was possible I might still be saved, but I doubted that. For one thing, I had no desire to turn to a deity with the intention of begging for help. That was being a fair-weather friend, and I just didn't do that shit. Plus, my father, who has lied to billions but never to me, has told me it makes no difference what spiritual path I follow. I could be a priest or an atheist for all he cared. I was still going to the same place when I died. He said human beings and demons have free will. I was neither, so I was shit out of luck in that department. Those are his exact words, by the way.

"Nick..."

I looked over at Vivian. She sat hunched in the passenger seat, one of our plastic shopping bags in her lap with the Curiosities logo on it. I had given her a list of things for her to gather from the shop if she wanted to learn to control the craft. Novice stuff. She had done so, and I'd made note of those things in the ledger so I could cover them with my wages. At least Morgana couldn't accuse me of ripping off the shop.

I eased back in my seat. "I'm sorry."

She looked very pretty sitting there. After she'd washed up, all her makeup had come off and she still looked amazing. She looked like a young Audrey Hepburn with red hair, the glowing innocence and the mysterious, almost Oriental cat eyes that worked so well together. Her lashes were long and dark, like a leopardess's. She must have known what I was thinking, because she set the bag down on the floor of the car and scooted into my lap. She slid her arms around me, up under my arms, and brushed her mouth against mine, inviting me to kiss her. I cupped the back of her head and plunged my tongue deep into her mouth. Vivian could be sweet as well as sexy. She kissed me while hugging me against her. It felt good to be held that way, like she needed me to protect her.

Finally, she said against my mouth, "Is your girlfriend angry with me, Nick?"

"She's not my girlfriend. She's my partner."

"But you live together."

"We cohabitate. The shop is holy ground. That prevents creatures like Malach from killing me."

She thought about that. "Do you have sex?" She said it not in some accusing way but like she was genuinely curious.

I found it very difficult to lie to Vivian. "Sometimes," I said. "But we're not a couple."

She looked at me earnestly. "I don't mind, you know."

"What's that?"

"I don't mind if you have sex with someone else. But I'd like to be your girl. I mean, your number one. Your girlfriend."

I looked at her in surprise. "You're like some guy's wet dream, do you know that, Vivian?"

She shrugged. Her eyes were much older than the rest of her, thousands of years, at least. "I'm just realistic. My roommate Brittany is all about commitments. She gets serious with every guy she does. You know, every guy is the *one*, but then he leaves her. I know it's hard for people to commit in this day and age."

She talked like someone who'd seen it all, who'd lived a hundred lifetimes. While she talked, her hand wandered to the fly of my jeans, where she pressed with unsubtle intent.

Her touch made me lurch in my seat. "How old were you when you lost your virginity?" I asked suddenly.

She held my eyes. She wasn't ashamed. "I was nine. And no, it wasn't consensual. My science teacher Mr. McCarty took advantage of me. He asked me to stay after school to help him with a project for the state fair and then he forced himself on me."

I felt a dull shock. "Did you report him?"

"No. When we were done, I realized I liked it a lot. We did it maybe a dozen more times over the school year until he lost interest. He was into the whole fear thing, and I wasn't afraid. He's probably still dicking little girls even today. It wouldn't surprise me."

She had undone my jeans and begun stroking me in that way she had. Then she lowered her head, her long red hair brushing over my lap, and licked me until I shivered. "Does it make me a bad person that I don't care what happens to him?" she asked. "That I don't care if he's still doing little girls?"

"No," I said. In that moment, I wouldn't have cared if she'd told me she'd committed capital murder. She was exquisite. Unbelievable. Everything I wanted. Everything I'd been waiting for. "But you should have told me," I said, my voice hitching in my throat.

She licked and kissed me some more. "Why?"

I watched her as she worked me slowly and inexorably up to climax. I could feel it building in the base of my spine. I pushed my shoulders back into the seat. I thrust up and up into her warm, wet, feral mouth.

She stopped and I groaned in frustration. "How old were you?" she finally asked.

I was finding it very difficult to formulate any coherent thoughts at the moment. "Sixteen and twenty-one," I said, grunting with the effort and clutching the back of her head. "Sixteen with a girl, twenty-one with a guy."

I waited for her to say something. Despite the big modern trend toward bisexuality, I've found there are many girls who don't like to know that.

But all she said was, "You waited."

"I just found it difficult to find partners because of the...peculiarities of my situation." I lurched as she pushed me closer to the edge, her teeth grazing me deliciously. "I feel like we shouldn't be doing this," I said as I undulated against her, forcing more of myself down her throat, following the pattern she had set forth.

Her eyes flickered up. "Why?" she asked when she'd let me go, a simple statement. "I like sex with you, Nick."

"I'm much older than I look."

"So am I." She turned all her attention back to tormenting me.

She certainly knew how to bring a guy. I grunted and dug my fingernails deep into the upholstery as I shuddered and came hard in her mouth. After she had exhausted me, she sat up and kissed me so I tasted myself in her mouth.

"I like being with you, Nick, and talking to you. I don't expect you to commit. I don't care who else you're fucking. I just hope we can continue to have sex, and talk, and I want you to teach me magic. That's all I want from you." She stared at me directly, challenging me to say something to that.

I tucked myself away, realizing I had no argument. She was being honest. How many girls are honest like that? I realized I'd likely give her anything she asked, even my soul if she wanted it. If she wanted to learn magic, I would teach her. If she wanted to have wild, no-commitment sex where neither of us was monogamous, I could do that too. At least, I hoped I could.

"You know that Mr. Fernstermacher likely saw us just now," I said.

She stroked my cheek with her fingertips. "You know, for the future ruler of hell, you're awful prudish."

I laughed and started the car.

\*\*\*

Vivian lived in a side-by-side family house on Baker's Lane, which was pretty funny when I thought about it, since she was studying to be a pastry chef. As we cruised down the tree-lined, suburban-perfect street, passing the occasional Saturday morning garage sale, Vivian told me about her roommate Brittany, about the classes she took, and her schedule. We decided that Tuesday, Wednesday and Friday nights would be best to work on her magic. She didn't work those evenings at the steakhouse and she had classes in the early morning. She was available Saturday and Sunday mornings as well, but the shop was busy on the weekend so that wouldn't work for me. I would teach her at her apartment in an effort to avoid Morgana.

She then asked me some personal questions, mostly about sex, what I liked and didn't like. I discovered that Vivian was very interested in the swinger lifestyle. She wanted to be in a solid relationship with someone she trusted, someone like me, but still be able to bring a third party in on occasion. She didn't mind doing it with a girl, though that wasn't her preference. She did want to see me do it with a guy. I think I was more embarrassed than she was. Sometimes the era I live in just boggles my mind.

She stopped talking when I slowed a few houses down from her place. There was a roadblock set up. I caught the flash of an ambulance up ahead, and a bad feeling seized me then, and apparently Vivian as well. She sat up straight and stared out of the windshield. "Fuck," she said, softly. She unclipped her seatbelt, jerked open the passenger side, and slid out while the car was still rolling along the asphalt.

I immediately hit the brake. "Viv—" I began, but she was already through the police blockade. I didn't know what else to do, so I simply shut off the car in the middle of the street and got out. I jogged after Vivian, stopping only when I saw her standing before her yellow, vinyl-sided, side-by-side.

A half dozen police cars and two ambulances were clustered in the street, and neighbors from across the street and various yard sales were gathering like curious crows. The front door of the side-by-side was open and police from two counties were filtering in and out. I spotted the coroner's car, then saw Deputy Branson taking a neighbor's statement. The moment he saw me, he raised a radio to his mouth. A few seconds later, Ben stepped out of the house and headed toward us, not hurrying but determined. He wore his square mirrored Super Trooper shades, and his mouth was set in a severe all-business line under his mustache.

More cops emerged from the house, and a few from cruisers parked somewhat randomly in the closed-off street. They too started toward us, as if to hem us in. As if we might bolt down the street when we had no idea what was going on.

Vivian took my hand in hers. She was shaking.

Ben had reached us. He gave me a dismissive look before turning his full attention on Vivian. I didn't let go of her hand, and I had to suppress the insane desire to shield Vivian with my body. "Ma'am, are you Vivian Summers?"

"Brittany," Vivian said. I saw real, white-faced shock on her face. "What's happened to Brittany?"

"I'm going to have to ask you to come with me," Ben said. "We need to ask you a few questions in regards to the murder of Brittany Bennett, ma'am."

Vivian turned white as sheet. I was afraid for a moment that she might pass out. Instead, she tried to push past Ben, to run to the house, but two officers from the Highway Patrol suddenly surrounded her and took her by both arms. They herded her toward Ben's patrol car.

I immediately started to intervene. I didn't care if they were officers of the law, I didn't want them touching Vivian that way, but Ben stepped in front of me and said in a low warning growl, "If you know what's good for you, Nick, you'll get the hell out of here *now*."

# | 10 |

SOMETIME BETWEEN TEN and eleven p.m. the night before, someone had taken a blunt weapon to the back of Brittany Bennett's skull. They had bludgeoned her until she was dead or unconscious, then driven her body out to the empty lot behind the local adult movie store, parked the car in a slot bordering the woods, and rolled the body down the incline until it landed in Buck's Creek. The whole thing had taken less than half an hour.

That's what the coroner told me, anyway, and he only did so because he owed me a favor. I had exorcised a low-level demon out his prize-winning Grande Poodle two years ago.

The coroner, Derrek Hambly, was still trying to determine if Brittany had died of the beating or because she had landed unconscious in the creek. The information was vital, because if Brittany's attacker had left her alive, and she had drowned after the fact, the perp would likely get life in prison without parole. If it could be proven that Brittany had died of her injuries, the perp was facing the very real possibility of Murder One and death row in the great Commonwealth of Pennsylvania.

Yes, we have the green mile here.

Either way, Brittany Bennett had still been very dead when an early-morning jogger had spotted her body. Three sets of fingerprints had been lifted from the inside of Brittany's abandoned car—

Brittany's, her boyfriend Mark's, and Vivian's. The murder weapon had not yet been found. Brittany's boyfriend Mark had been the natural first selection for a suspect, but he had a solid alibi: he'd been busy bagging two girls from Scranton at the time. Lucky for Mark, he also filmed it.

That left Vivian as a suspect—Vivian who had no alibi. She'd gotten off shift at Molly's Steakhouse at nine o'clock the night before, had come straight home, changed, and started out to see me, confident that all the Saturday night activity on the Strip would be enough to keep Malach at bay. It hadn't. Vivian had wound up taking shelter under the Jehovah's Witnesses' eaves for over twenty minutes before he'd finally given up and left. She'd explained about her stalker, but the police were dubious at best. The whole situation had left her a perfect window of opportunity to kill Brittany, and no alibi until she'd seen me at quarter to eleven.

I thanked Derrek and borrowed his office for ten minutes. Derrek's computer was connected to the NCIC, the criminal database maintained by the FBI that was not made available to the private sector. Derrek, though a very good coroner, was also a Luddite. I wasn't at all surprised to find that he used auto logins for everything because he couldn't remember his passwords. Auto logins are bad if you have a computer that anyone can access. It means people like me can look at your shit. Remember that.

In less than five minutes, I'd discovered that Vivian Summers had a criminal record longer than my arm. I was mildly surprised but not overly offended. I wasn't exactly an angel, either. Derrek's printer spat out the last of Vivian's criminal record, and I slid it neatly into a manila folder.

Derrek chose that moment to step back into his office. He looked horrified. "Look, man, I owe you big. But I don't owe you *that* big. You're gonna get me fired here!"

"I wasn't here."

"Nick!"

"Not one word or I put the demon back."

Derrek shut up.

\* \* \*

There was a nice little picnicking spot on the shore of Indian Mountains Lake Park. It's far enough in that you can park and have some privacy, but not too far that you get eaten alive by insects in the summer months. I sometimes went there to meditate at the edge of the water. I'm not very good at meditation. I always wind up wondering if I put my coat in the washer or if I dropped it off at the dry cleaners. I'd hoped to bring Vivian there one day soon. I'd had admittedly romantic notions about teaching her magic in the forest and making love to her down by the water, but I wasn't sure if that was going to happen now.

I thought I loved her, but I wasn't utterly blinded by that love. I wasn't stupid in love. I wasn't stupid, period. I had to get to the bottom of this mess. So I drove to my favorite spot, sat down by the water's edge, drank my Chai tea from Starbucks, and read over Vivian's criminal record, which was fairly extensive and read like a Stephen King novel.

My cell went off but I ignored it. I knew it was Morgana, but I wasn't prepared to deal with her at the moment.

Vivian was adopted and had lived most of her life in White Haven. A lawyer, Stan Summers, and his barren second wife, Kathy, had adopted Vivian when she was only a baby. She had come from an orphanage in Philadelphia. Last night, while we lay in bed, Vivian had alluded to parents who had died in a car accident two years ago, but she hadn't said she was adopted. Maybe she was too young to think of herself as adopted. Or maybe she didn't want me knowing.

There was nothing about Mr. McCarty, her science teacher. She was, however, brought up on assault charges while in junior high. A janitor named Joseph Greeley had attacked Vivian, but she had managed to push him down a long flight of stairs. The janitor wound up paralyzed from the waist down. He blew his brains out the back of his skull before he could be transferred to an Administrative Minimum Security Prison for the mentally ill. Before he'd died, he'd left a note stating that he knew the name of the Antichrist and that he walked the earth as a man, seeking whom he might devour. He cited Vivian as the Whore of Babylon, the consort of the Antichrist, and stated that he wished to rid the world of her.

Overall, a standup guy. Very imaginative.

Vivian had a long list of misdemeanor charges after that—shoplifting; assault on a police officer; assault on another minor (she punched a girl at a Papa Roach concert); and seven traffic violations for speeding/running a red light/failing to stop at a stop sign. The misdemeanor charges were excessive but not weird or unusual. It was pretty obvious that Vivian had had a rough time growing up.

It wasn't until she was eighteen that the big kahuna raised its head. That's when she was charged with arson on an apartment building in downtown Bethlehem. Several people who escaped the blaze claimed they saw Vivian that night, standing *inside* the flames, untouched. The fire was found to have originated in the apartment of Vivian's then-boyfriend Mitchell. It was estimated to have burned at approximately nine hundred degrees—roughly the afterburner of a jet plane.

To give you an idea of how hot that is, even bone had been incinerated. Twelve people died in the fire, including two children. The intensity of the fire had burned the building down to its plumbing in less than ten minutes. Some chemicals had been found in Mitchell's apartment—he worked as a plumbing assistant—but nothing that could be proven to be an accelerant for a fire of that intensity. The coroner had had to identify Mitchell by a handful of molars.

Again, Vivian was not charged. Not enough evidence. The fire was blamed on an underground chemical leak. Shortly afterward, she moved out of her parents' place and moved here to her apartment in Blackwater. Her parents, already estranged from her, refused to speak to her at all. Not long after, they both died in a hit-and-run.

I lowered the printout in my hand and noticed Brownswick sitting beside me, knees bent and hand scratching at his beard in perfect imitation of me. His antlers, stretching like two huge branches in an upward direction, were full of fall leaves, shining pollen, and dandelion fluff. A yellow jacket buzzed lazily around his ears, then buzzed away.

"Hello, Little Horn," he said when I had acknowledged him. "Did you find the lost girl?"

"No," I said, sounding surly.

He snorted, blowing pollen out of his nostrils and onto my coat. I shook it off. "You've mated with the female daemon."

I had showered well this morning. The fact that he could detect that was annoying. "And this is your business…how?"

He touched his heart dramatically. "You wound me, Lord of Flies. Your business is my business."

"Those names you use get annoying after a while."

"You are being a smart ass," he said. Except he said the word wrong, like two words. It was obvious he'd picked the slang up somewhere. "But that is your right, Willful King."

I shuffled some papers in my hands. "Get to the point, Brownie."

Brownswick smiled. It was, as usual, a mischievous smile. "Why did you not bring the female daemon to the woods? I desire to meet her." He sounded cartoonishly wounded. I knew better. He just wanted to chase Vivian through the trees.

"The police have her for questioning. They think she committed a crime."

"You certainly know how to choose a mate."

"Is there some point to you bothering me, Brownie?"

Brownswick moved closer to me. I moved further away from him. The last thing I needed was to smell like faun. "My wives tell me the trees have seen a girl, but they do not know if it is the girl you seek. The trees do not see well."

I sighed. Ben had seen to it that I was off this case, so I didn't know why I even cared. I had more than enough on my mind at the moment. "Do they know where she is?"

"They tell me north, in the great woods."

"That's not especially helpful."

"Near a place where the bees are thick and plentiful. The trees do not know what the girl looked like. They were too busy shedding leaves."

"The trees aren't very helpful. I need a landmark, Brownie, not some prosaic bullshit."

"The trees said to follow the bees. The bees know the girl."

I wanted to facepalm, but I smiled at Brownie instead. There was no sense in pissing off the trees. I've seen trees *move*. Don't think they can't do it. "Please thank the trees for me and tell them to keep an eye out for the girl."

"They said they would do that. The trees like children." Then Brownswick looked at me with genuine interest. "What will you do about the female daemon?"

"Prove her innocence, of course."

"*Is* she innocent, my Lord?"

"I just don't know, Brownie."

* * *

Around four, I had formulated a plan of action, so to speak, but I had to see Vivian. It was vitally important.

They were holding her at the county jail, her bail set unreasonably high. I suppose they thought she might run. A public defender had been there already, thankfully. I went in, was relieved to see that Ben wasn't around, and requested permission to speak to her.

The guard on duty led me into the visiting room, a cold little box painted a dismal grey. It was partitioned in half by a wall, and cut into the walls were little windows barely large enough to see a person. The windows were bulletproof glass with a small slit cut in the bottom only big enough to slide your hand. There were guards on both sides, watching. I sat down in the cold metal folding chair in front of one of the windows and waited.

A few minutes later, a tall, black, female guard led Vivian out. Her name was Bunny Killborn. No, really. That's her name. Her real name. I nodded to Bunny. Bunny nodded back, all business-like. Bunny does not suffer fools gladly, probably because of the razzing she most certainly received in school because of her name. I could respect that.

"Nick," Vivian said. Bunny led her to the window and she sat down and faced me through the glass partition. We didn't have phones like in crime movies. Something like that was not in the micro-budget in a place like Bucks County, Pennsylvania.

"Vivian," I said. I kept my voice neutral. "You all right?

She looked around the room, then at me. "No. They're holding me for some ridiculous bail money. They think I killed Brittany. Are you here to investigate what really happened?"

"Not in any official capacity. There's really nothing I can do." I saw her face fall. "I mean, officially. But I will help you, if I can." I closed my eyes and gathered myself. "I'm going to ask you a series of questions. I need you to answer them for me, without qualifying them."

She looked confused. "I guess."

"No qualifying and no explanations. Just a simple response. This is very important, Vivian."

"All right." She looked at me direly through the glass.

I licked my dry lips and said, "Why didn't you tell me you were adopted?"

"I don't understand what this has to do with anything, Nick."

"I need these answers from you, Vivian. Answer the question."

She flinched. I was using my Interrogation Voice, which I hadn't used since I left the force over five years ago. Peter always let me interview suspects. He liked how I was able to drag the most ridiculous shit out of people. "I didn't tell you because it happened so long ago, before I could even remember. Besides, my parents are dead now."

Good enough, and what I had expected. I moved on to the next question. "Why did you hurt the janitor who attacked you in junior high?"

Vivian blanched noticeably, then immediately composed herself. "He attacked me."

"So did Mr. McCarty."

"No, McCarty was different. He seduced me. Greeley attacked me. He meant to hurt me. He said I was evil."

I nodded at that. I'd heard variations on that theme all of my life. Some people could just naturally feel daemons out, I think. It made me trust people a little bit less. Next question. "Why did you attack that girl at the concert?"

"She called me a witch."

I waited.

"She'd started dating my boyfriend at the time." Vivian looked annoyed. "Both answers are true, Nick."

Next. "Have you ever willfully committed a crime? Let's say a misdemeanor like shoplifting."

She looked me straight in the eye. "Yes."

"Have you ever committed a minor felony, like boosting a car?"

"Yes."

Bunny stood at the far end of the room. I pitched my voice low. "Did you kill your boyfriend Mitchell?" There was no way Bunny could hear my whisper—and no way for Vivian to incriminate herself.

I waited.

Vivian blanched further. "How do you know about Mitchell?"

"Answer the question or I leave now."

I saw the war in her face. Finally, she said, "Yes."

"Qualify that."

"It was an accident. I didn't mean to hurt him. I loved him."

"He was cheating on you?"

Vivian clasped her hands together and stared down at her chipped and bitten fingernails. "Yes."

"How did you kill him?"

Vivian's eyes flickered. "We were angry. Shouting. Mitchell caught fire."

"You set him on fire?"

"No, Mitchell just caught fire. I don't know how, but I know I caused it."

I waited, allowing her to recover from the questions. I could see it hurt her deeply, and that gave me some reassurances. A truly evil person would not care. An evil person would have no remorse. I was starting to believe that Morgana, and the janitor who tried to hurt Vivian, were wrong. Vivian might love sex and drugs—she might even have stolen cars—but that did not make her evil.

I spoke low. "Did you and Brittany share any boyfriends?"

She looked up then, worriedly. "Yes."

"Your last? Mark?"

"Yes."

"Were you still seeing him?"

"No." She sat up straight then and pinned me with a determined look. "I wanted to see *you*, Nick. You know that. I wanted *you*, not him."

"Did you kill Brittany, Vivian?"

"No!"

"Why were your fingerprints found in Brittany's car?"

"I drove Brittany's car sometimes." She let out her breath in a near-desperate gasp. "My car is in the shop. I drove her car to school yesterday."

"That's all the questions I have."

"I didn't kill Brittany, Nick," Vivian said. There was real pain in her eyes now. That and panic. She grabbed my hand through the slit in the window. "I loved Brittany. I loved her more than that shithead she was screwing. I wouldn't hurt her for *him*. Mark was fucking everything in the county. He's not worth it."

"I believe you," I told her, holding her hand. "I believe you and I'll find a way to prove you're innocent. I'll get you out of here."

"I don't care about that."

"You should," I told her. I glanced around, careful the guard wasn't watching. "This place isn't holy ground, Vivian. Malach could come for you at any time."

"I don't care, Nick. I don't care if I die. I only care about Josh."

I stopped and stared long and hard at her. "Josh?"

She looked desperate. "Do you have a pen and paper? They won't let me having anything here."

I dug out my notebook and Vivian dictated a name and an address to me. I looked at it.

Vivian said, "Josh is my brother...my adopted brother. He's older. My dad had him with his first wife. He took care of me a lot of the time. We took care of each other after our parents died. He's the only family I have left now. He's a musician. He plays the Philly circuit."

"You want me to call him for you?"

"I want you to protect him, Nick." Her hands tightened on mine. "If Malach has arranged this, he might go after Josh next."

I shook my head. "That's not how this system works, Vivian. Malach's scary but he doesn't incriminate innocent people. And he can't kill human beings. There are rules."

"What if he broke the rules? What if there are no rules?"

I gave her a sympathetic look. Malach was a mercenary—no argument about that—but he was still a Seraph. He had his marching orders.

"Vivian," I tried to explain. "You and I...we're unnatural creatures. But we still have to follow rules. My dad has to follow them. Malach certainly has to follow them."

She glared at me. "Angels have to be behind it, Nick. There is no one else who would do this to me."

"Are you sure? There's Greeley and Mitchell. That's reason enough for someone to want to hurt you. Even McCarty, if he thinks you might talk."

"You think someone's carrying around a vendetta? All that happened years ago." She sat back in her seat and rubbed her tired eyes.

"Jesus, this is like a bad TV cop movie. I used to laugh at episodes of *Columbo* that did things like this."

"I won't let any angels hurt you," I told her. "I can put a temporary spell around the building to prevent Malach from entering."

"And Josh?" She leaned forward, her face strained, and for once, unpretty. "He was in Afghanistan, Nick. He lost his sight there. I need you to find him and protect him. You can't let Malach—or whoever—get him. *Please.*"

"I'll do whatever I can."

# | 11 |

I WAS HEADED south, toward the Pennsylvania Turnpike, when I realized I had some unfinished business to take care of. It was unseasonably warm and I had the windows down, the hot, leafy air filtering into the car as I passed the rocky, still-green Lehigh Mountains. Pennsylvania is as famous for its Indian Summers as it is for its fall foliage. It usually stays hot and almost airless up until the middle of November—then, *bam*, instant winter. More snow days than you can shake your frozen ass at.

By my estimation, it would take at least an hour and a half to get to the outskirts of Philly, and by then it would be well past six o'clock, the time when I usually took over the shop from Morgana.

I dug out my cell phone. Morgana had since left two more messages. I called her cell and she picked up on the second ring. "Where the hell are you?"

"I'm on my way to Philly."

"Reason?"

"Personal."

"Well, fuck you, too."

Morgana almost never swore. I had really pissed her off this time. I thought about handing her a story, but I knew she'd learn what was going on with Vivian before the end of the day, and she'd *know* it had something to do with my sudden disappearance. In a town like Blackwater, rumor spreads faster than a bad case of the clap. I gave her a synopsis of what had happened since I left the loft. She wasn't overly impressed.

"She's a daemon, Nick. She's more than capable of murder. And don't start with that racist shit. You know I'm right. Hell, you just told me she killed one of her boyfriends."

"Vivian can kill people. But she didn't kill Brittany."

"Are you sure?"

"Yes. She's being set up."

"And you're going to find out who's behind it all."

"No, I'm going to Philly to collect her brother and bring him back to Blackwater where I can keep an eye on him. Vivian has a public defender for the charges. The prosecutor is still putting together a case, but nothing is going to move until they find a murder weapon. I put a spell on the county jail to keep Malach out for now. That's all I can do."

"You haven't talked to Sheriff Ben yet?" She sounded surprised.

"Ben's pissed off with me."

"How about that coroner friend of yours? Can't he help?"

"Derrek's not going to want to see me either."

"Is there anyone you have *not* pissed off today yet?"

"None that I can think of."

There was a long pause as I turned off the highway and into a Wawa to refill. "I'll take the shop tonight," Morgana finally told me. "But you're doing a full shift tomorrow, Scratch."

"Deal."

"I'm still pissed off with you."

"I know," I said as I parked in front of a pump and turned off the car. I thought about apologizing, but what was I going to say? *Sorry, Morgana, I tried to strangle you?* Oh, hell...

"Morgana...I'm sorry I tried to strangle you."

There was a long pause as Morgana contemplated that. "I told Anton about the angel dolls. He said a member of his coven has books on reverse conjuring."

That was essentially Morgana accepting my apology. I felt a burden lift. "What the hell is reverse conjuring?"

"It's the same as demonic conjuring, except with angels."

"You're kidding me. Angel magic?" I said in disbelief as I got out of the car and filled up. Angel magic in the occult community is a little like the chupacabra or the Loch Ness Monster.

Everyone knows someone who knows someone who's seen it done, but no one can prove it. In angel magic, a powerful witch supposedly has the power to call upon and control angels, which is patently ridiculous and impossible and bends every natural, and unnatural, law. Angels cannot be controlled except by the Throne. Angel magic is bullshit, and you can quote me on that. I said as much to Morgana.

"Anton's friend has an old Book of Shadows from a witch who was hanged during the Salem trials. He said the book has illustrations that look a lot like the angel dolls. Problem is, it's in some other language. Do you want us to work on translating it?"

I thought about that as I hung the pump back up. I had serious doubts that it would help in the disappearance of Cassie Berger, but I saw no reason to turn down free information. Anyway, I had to admit I was a little curious about Angel Magic. "Yes. Please. Let me know if anything looks interesting."

"Good enough. Take care of yourself, Scratch."

"You too." I slipped the cell into my jeans pocket and visited the Wawa for a giant-sized Diet Dr. Pepper and a new pack of Camels. I estimated that was enough caffeine for the remaining seventy-five miles to Philly. I also bought some more M&Ms and a package of Swedish Fish. Yes, I know. If I wasn't half demon, I would be fat, pimply, and crippled by COPD and diabetes.

The overweight, middle-aged, desperate-looking counter girl took my money with shaking hands. Her washed-out blue eyes went huge in her head as she checked me out. "Oh, my God, you're gorgeous!" she exclaimed. "I have a back room. You wanna fuck, beautiful?"

I shook my head and left. Only in PA.

\* \* \*

Mostly, I hate Philadelphia. It reminds me of New York, just poorer and more desperate. You either have glass and granite skyscrapers or disintegrating row houses, and sometimes you have them all mixed up on the same street, along with plenty of saggy high-tension wires and turn-of-the-century streetlights, like the city can't figure out what era it's in. Also, I've tried to go native and get behind the Phillies, I really have, but they've only ever won two World Series and just plain suck and you know it. They're like the East Coast answer to the Cubbies. Still, that's a rant for another day.

As soon as I was inside the city limits, I pulled into a slot in the parking lot of a Quickie Mart and went over the Yahoo maps I keep in the glove compartment. I have a big stack of them covering New York, New Jersey, and Pennsylvania, marking where various churches and synagogues are located. It never hurts to know where to go, should I run into a Seraph or soldier angel. It took a while, but I managed to pinpoint The Chicken Coop on South Street, where Josh Summers was playing a gig tonight at eight o'clock.

The sun had gone down, so at least I didn't have to look at the city, just its lights as I drove toward South Street. I was finally out of Dr. Pepper, I had chain-smoked the pack down, and I had chocolaty peanut debris stuck in my back molars. I still had the Swedish Fish, though, so all was well.

I found the place tucked between a greasy spoon and an antique shop. As a rule of thumb, every major retail and recreational strip in the state of Pennsylvania has an antique shop on it, and they are almost never open. If you don't believe me, find the nearest antique shop in your area of PA and drive by it as often as you can. You'll see it's always closed and never moves any merchandise. I'm fairly convinced that the New York Mafia owns most of the antique shops in PA and just uses them to launder money. A useless tangent, but I felt it warranted mentioning.

The club mentioned no charge, but I did have to feed the meter in order to park on the street. Inside, the place was narrow and long and almost pitch black. It looked like every redneck bar I'd ever seen in Blackwater. It had a pinball machine, two pool tables, and a jukebox. The only thing different was that it had a slightly raised dais separated from the rest of the room by a wall of chicken wire where the visiting talent was encouraged to play. The place sported all the usual suspects—retirees, alcoholics, older female divorcees, a scattering of overweight nerds who couldn't get girls. Not exactly the kind of clientele to warrant a riot barrier, so I had to assume the chicken wire was there as part of some ongoing theme.

The musician onstage was sitting down with a steel guitar across his lap. He was playing an amazing cover of "Hellhound on my Trail," which I considered a very bad omen. He was a big guy, and he had a lot of muscle going on. His dirty blond hair fell to his chin and he sported a hippie goatee. He sang unhurriedly in a scorched, whiskey-saturated voice and the people in the audience, drunk or otherwise, nodded in rhythm and appreciation. After all, it was just one of those songs.

Down in the front, two guys sat at a table, doing nothing at all. They were the only ones not drinking or following the music. They were just staring at the musician. That would have been suspicious anyway you looked at it, but they were also dressed in a lot of dusty black leather like a big pair of gay biker dudes.

The thing about angels is, they're a little bit like Cthulhu and the Outer Gods. Unless the Throne has assigned them to you, they only became aware of your presence when you become aware of theirs. You have to know them for what they are, and you really have to believe to get their attention.

Unfortunately, I believed. A lot.

Almost immediately, the pair of angels turned their heads as they became aware of my presence. They were big and blond. I don't think an angel exists that is not. They had long pale hair and icy blue eyes. Any difference between them was dictated solely by their function. Soldier angels, for instance, have huge hands to better grip weaponry. Messenger angels have longer legs in order to travel faster. These angels had big hands, so I doubted they were here with trumpets and good tidings.

They stood up together, in perfect sync. Gotta love the coordination. One angel lifted his big hand and folded down his two middle fingers, then said some archaic words in angel speech. I felt a funny, sickening lurch in my stomach as I realized they were casting a spell, literally stopping time in its tracks in order to deal with their Eternal Enemy without disturbing the humans' perception of their world. The people in the bar immediately froze in whatever position they were in. The bartender, who'd been pulling a Budweiser draft, froze up with a long, sparkling amber arc of beer flowing into a glass. It was almost cool.

The other angel reached into some secret slot in his leather biker coat and pulled forth an impossibly long golden sword with a lot of angel hieroglyphs along the blade. The blade of the sword was as tall as I am. Both of them looked at me and said, as one in a booming baritone, "Greetings, Little Horn. We must kill you now."

God, I fucking hate angels.

# | 12 |

I REALIZED THE jig was up and things were about to get messy.

I've always wanted to write that, ever since I read my first hardboiled detective novel. Anyway, the jig *was* up, and I was left staring down two very pissed off angels who knew who and what I was. So things were indeed likely to get very messy in the next few minutes.

Let me see if I can put this in a way you'll dig. A dictator attacks the United States of America pretty much unprovoked. The President leads a return assault on the dictator's home soil. The two armies engage in some pretty bloody fighting that lasts years and costs millions of Americans their lives. It's brutal and changes the landscape of America. Then one day, a couple of Navy Seals guys who've seen years of combat are sitting in a sleazy bar when they recognize the dictator's son sitting at another table. I mean, this thing could only end one way.

I really couldn't blame the angels when they charged me. Still, I didn't like it when the first angel grabbed me by the throat with his big hand, cutting off my breath, and the other one started laying into me. He sucker punched me first in the ribs and then in the kidneys. Even though I knew he hadn't driven his fist all the way through my body, it certainly felt that way. Suddenly it was impossible to breathe, I felt like I was going to throw up, and I knew I was going to pass out. Then these two chumps would drag me before the Throne at their leisure.

The first angel threw me down. That woke me up. Then the two of them started really going at me *Casino*-style. I buckled down, trying to make a smaller target of myself, but they managed to get in some really good kicks. It hurt like hell and, after a minute or so, I could taste blood frothing into my mouth. They were good, but I'd been beat up by punks on New York crack, and that's like getting a smackdown by the Big Boss at the end of the video game. You wonder how you'll ever survive it, and you wonder if you even want to. Jesus, my face looked like ground hamburger the following day after one such punk got ahold of me.

Coiling my legs, I kicked out, nailing one of the angels in the ankles.

He went down hard and I rolled over. I reached out and touched him. Immediately, all my unholy un-goodness infected his perfect, pearly white skin, and it began to burn. The angel screamed so loudly that my hearing went out for a second. That's some powerful screaming.

I rolled to my feet, and almost right into the sword swing of the second angel. It came down hard, splitting the floor in front of me. I dodged left. He followed my motion. He swung his sword around, but it was big and awkward and slowed him down. He was close enough for me to side-kick him in the belly. I am not without kung fu, courtesy of the New York Police Academy. I felt about a dozen hurting muscles rip and tear as I did so, but it felt so good to watch him go down like a brick wall.

His sword flew back into the table behind him, flattening it, while the patrons in their timelock continued to stare at the musician on the stage, oblivious to what was happening around them.

We were all operating inside about a tenth of a microsecond, so what they didn't know couldn't hurt them.

The first angel had recovered. He came up behind me and grabbed my arms, pulling me back against him, presumably so his partner could finish kicking the shit out of me. I didn't plan to wait that long. I smashed the back of my head against his face. I'd learned that in Jackie Chan movies, by the way. It hurt but it did its job. It knocked the angel off balance, and the two of us toppled back, landing on the floor between the tables. My angel took the full impact with a cough of breath. I spun around, holding him down with my weight, and pop-punched him in the mouth before jumping up and back.

The second angel's sword came chopping down, hacking into the table beside me and perilously close to his partner. A couple of Budweiser glasses went crashing to the floor. If I hadn't been moving, the blade would have found itself *inside* me. The blade, covered in arcane symbols designed to harm the fallen, would have hurt like hell. The second angel tried to pull his sword loose, but he'd lodged it in there pretty good, sort of like Excalibur.

I shifted away from both angels in a way that I could keep them both in my line of sight. I spit blood. "Yahtzee," I said.

The second angel turned and looked at me with his mechanical blue eyes. Pale blue blood drooled from his mouth where I'd done a good job busting up his teeth some. He licked at it. "Always with the funnies, Little Horn."

"I'm a pretty funny guy," I told him as I drew the Tanaka from my armpit holster. It wouldn't hurt these guys much but it gave me a false sense of security. I even turned it sideways just so I could feel more gangsta. "But you guys never notice because you're always too busy trying to kill me."

"If we kill the young Lucifer, the Father of Lies will have no heirs. His kingdom will fall to ruin."

"Unless my dad goes out and dicks another girl." The angels stopped and stared at me in a blank way, then looked at each other. Of course, I really didn't expect creatures born with no genitalia to have their minds in the gutter like me. "Didn't think of that, did you?"

While they were contemplating that, I considered taking a bead on their bellies. Angels, demons and daemons have two hearts, one in their chest and a second sacred heart in their bellies, put there by their Creator to give them magic. If you can destroy their second heart, you can kill the magic—and, thus, the being in question. I don't make up the rules; I just follow them. Still, I figured it was pretty likely the two angels were wearing protective gear under their clothes to protect their sacred hearts. If I shot at them and it bounced off their armor, it would give them a great big bellyache, and then they'd be even angrier with me. You had to know how to pick your fights.

A sudden motion caught my attention onstage. The musician—likely Josh—was on his feet, standing with the steel guitar hanging around his middle. He had his fingers hooked in the steel mesh of the chicken wire and he was turning his head, trying to follow what was going on. I found it interesting that Josh wasn't stuck in the timelock like the patrons of the bar. That meant the angels had planned on doing business with him. Probably very bad business. While the two angels considered their next move, I called to Josh and told him to head for the back door.

"Who are you?" he said finally. His voice was hoarse and made me want to clear my throat. He turned to follow my voice.

"Your sister sent me!" I said. "Get to the back door *now*!"

Josh was a smart man. He turned toward a door at the back of the stage.

I heard a headache-inducing roar behind me. I turned. I beheld the two angels.

They had both finally decided on their next move.

Both had torn away their human disguises completely. Both were Cherubim, I realized—not hit men like Malach, but more like Special Ops Navy Seals. I wish I could say they were cute little winged babies, but those are putti, or cupids, and those are images found in Italian Renaissance and Baroque art. Cherubim are giant golden creatures with the bodies of lions, the faces of humans, and four wings each. For angels, they are ugly as all get-out, scary as hell, and they make you want to wash your eyeballs in vinegar. Seriously.

The two Cherubim sprang at me, roaring.

I didn't even bother trying to aim the gun, not that it would do me any good anyway. I raised both hands in a defensive gesture and *pushed* my will out at them. As a witch, I'm unique in that I don't need magical paraphernalia or even spells to do magic. I don't even really need to know what I'm doing. I'm sort of the equivalent of a magical idiot savant. I just need to *want* something. I need motivation. It's probably the same principal as when Vivian set fire to Mitchell. It's not that she probably hated him, or that she even wanted to do it, but that she was angry. Anger is a powerful motivator, as is fear.

I knew the Cherubim pouncing at me could tear me apart. I knew they could eat my second heart. I knew they could kill me. And I did not want to die. Sue me.

My will caused a rippling distortion in the air, like heat off a deadpan desert. The Cherubim hit it and bounced, flying the whole length of the room. One crashed into the far wall, ripping down posters on the community board. The other hit the jukebox. It rattled side to side, lit up, and Alan Jackson started singing, "Don't Rock the Jukebox" before it shorted out and went dark.

That was me, by the way.

The Cherubim recovered almost at once, shaking their heads to clear them, and started creeping toward me again, snarling out of their human mouths. Considering the amount of older people here, I calculated about a third of them would have suffered a coronary embolism at the sight of the monsters were they not stuck in time-lock. Lucky them.

One of the Cherubim stayed to the fore of me while the other crawled away into the dark like a giant cat. I knew that one meant to circle around. I knew they meant to box me in. They would attack me from both sides until they'd worn me down.

I have some fairly unique talents, but as a daemon, I'm also limited. I couldn't do this forever. But I knew one trick they'd love.

I watched the one in front of me prepare to pounce again. I saw the moment it coiled its back legs to spring. I also sensed the one behind me was already in motion. I did a kind of impromptu "Johnny B. Goode" sliding drop to the floor, sans guitar, and summoned a gate. The first Cherub had already cleared my head, but the second one leaped right into it, and I heard the echo of its roar as it fell through the equivalent of an earthbound wormhole.

I lowered my hands. I shut the door above me. As a general rule of thumb, it's unwise to leave a gateway to hell open for more than a few seconds. Something might come through.

The first Cherub landed on its haunches. It whipped around to face me, its human expression savage. "What did you do?" it roared.

"I sent your buddy away."

"Where?"

I smiled. "To my father's world. He's going to have a hell of a party."

Enraged, the remaining Cherub roared and leaped at me. I moved aside at the last second and the Cherub sailed right into the chicken wire, ripped through it like tissue paper, and kept going, crashing into all the sound equipment scattered around the back of the stage. There was a great deal of awesome electricity and fire, and plenty of smoke. I knew I had to move fast. The Cherub might be too injured to maintain the timelock spell. Then I'd have to deal with the chaos of people running willy-nilly everywhere, screaming about fire and monsters.

I lurched up on the stage, slid out of my coat, and beat out the flames. Then I moved to the back, my gun drawn and a hand over the place where my ribs were busted up pretty good. I can heal myself, but it takes time, and I need a quiet place to work. There was so much smoke, it was hard to see through it all, but I finally recognized an inert form lying beside a merrily burning amp. I kicked the burning amp away.

The Cherub had resumed his humanoid form. He lay on his back, clutching his belly where a microphone stand was protruding from it. Pale blue blood slicked his hands and was splashed across the floor. Talk about shitty luck. I went down on one knee beside the fallen angel. I kept my gun drawn but I didn't think I would need it now. "Sorry this happened, friend. I really would have liked to have avoided this."

The Cherub groaned and clawed at the obstruction in his heart slowly killing him.

"Who sent you?" I asked.

He shook his head from side to side. Long blond hair stuck to the blood on his face.

Angels are extremely loyal. They'd rather die than reveal their secrets. Goodie.

I reached down and grasped his bloody hand. The touch of my hand immediately infected him and he groaned, his back arching.

A kind of purplish leprosy started crawling up his hand and into his sleeve. The hand suddenly felt warm and feverish, and the skin began stinking like roadkill left to cook in the July sun. Blue blood bubbled in a froth over his lips. His body jerked almost orgasmically, but I knew he wasn't enjoying this in the least.

The pained, helpless look on the angel's face made me grin. "I can make this last a long, long time, friend. I can make you rot from the inside."

The angel gritted his teeth. "D-devil."

"Yeah, yeah. Tell me something I don't know." I tightened my hold on him and he began to scream almost piteously as his flesh began burning away under my hand. His flesh turned hot and kind of mushy and started looking like taco filling. I held on.

I leaned over him. I could smell the burning on him. "Who sent you here?"

It wasn't until his hand had burned down to a ragged skeleton that he finally began to talk. Even angels have their pain thresholds. This guy had found his. He said it was Gabriel who had sent him. Gabriel wanted the blind musician, Joshua Summers.

"What does he want with Josh?" I asked coolly. His hand was gross, but it wasn't hurting me in the least.

"T-to...kill him."

"Gabriel means to kill Josh?"

The angel nodded urgently. Like I was going to release my hold on him. Yeah, right.

"Gabriel can't kill Josh," I said, hoping I was right. "Even Archangels don't have Dominion over human beings."

The angel began to laugh almost hysterically. "They do now, devil."

I watched the angel's face. He was in too much pain to lie effectively. Anyway, angels can't lie. They could torture me, kill me, but they couldn't lie to me. "That's ridiculous. What does the Throne think of this turn of events?"

The angel shook his head, threshing his sweaty blond hair from side to side. "The Throne is empty," he finally admitted. "There is no Dominion...no Grace...no rules..." He continued to laugh hysterically. He showed his big white, blue-blood-coated teeth.

I looked at him critically. "God's stepped down?"

He didn't answer that. With his free hand he'd begun clawing at the steel that protruded from his heart. "We can hunt the daemons with impunity. Heaven has closed its doors...the rest is a battleground. You won't survive it, Little Horn...and neither will she..."

"Why is Gabriel interested in Vivian?"

Instead of answering, angel managed to push the rod of metal farther into his stomach with one hard thrust. I sensed the exact moment when his heart burst from the impact. A freshet of blue blood gushed over the angel's pale lips, then he shook all over and lay still. The hand I held began to soften. I let it go and stood back, watching as the angel's body charred and disintegrated in fast forward, even as the blood spattered on the floor. Within seconds, all I had was a microphone stand lying in a pile of dust—dust that was even now beginning to stir, it was so fine. I knew that within minutes that too would vanish so that no trace of the angel was left behind.

I sat on the floor and tried to recover. I found one more cigarette in the crumpled pack in my jacket. I lit it.

Heaven had closed its doors. There was no more Grace, no more forgiveness for sin. The angels were able to hunt my kind with impunity. Hell, the angels could hunt human beings without repercussions. God had stepped down and left us to our own devices. That meant the Earth was finally, truly, a battleground between angels, demons, humans, and those like myself and Vivian who walked between the worlds.

Well, fuck.

\* \* \*

I made it backstage to the dressing room in record time. In a shitty little honky-tonk like this, that meant a little area partitioned off with crates that was part of the larger storage area for the bar's liquor. A single naked bulb illuminated the cramped little room where some amps, guitars, and one of those cheap rollout sofas filled the space. All the comforts of home.

Josh Summers stood by the back door with a guitar case in one hand and a leash in the other. No suitcase or gym bag for his clothes. Good to know the guy had his priorities straight. The leash he held was attached to an absolutely humongous Rottweiler who sat on the floor, panting his guts out. Lovely. I wasn't exactly at the top of the Christmas card list when it came to animals.

I stopped within twenty feet of Josh. The dog had stood up and begun belly growling at me.

"Easy, Tiger," Josh said.

Had he really named a Rottweiler *Tiger*?

"Who are you?" Josh said.

I noticed he didn't mention if Tiger would attack me or not. I stayed put anyway. In my present hurty state, I was in no mood to wrestle a Rottweiler.

"Your sister Vivian sent me," I told him, sounding hoarser than I'd expected. I didn't like the way my mouth felt swollen and full of blood. I moved my hand around under my coat, pressing against various bad places, hoping my magic would hurry up and heal me already. I thought about saying, "You're in trouble. Some bad guys are after you," but then realized that Josh would expect clarification on that point. Instead, I decided to act on my instincts and said, "Josh, your sister is in trouble."

Josh shook his head. "Why didn't she call me?"

"She didn't want you involved."

"And you do?"

"You need to know what's going on," I said to deflect him. "And we need to get out of here *now*." With the second angel dead—who, it appeared, was the magic wielder—the spell that held the time-lock was going to start unraveling. Fast. When a time-lock spell starts to do that, it means the magician who laid the spell—in this case, the Cherub—is dead. That's significant because when an angel dies, it creates a kind of sonic pulse. Other angels can sense that pulse and they usually waste no time investigating. Hope you're following me so far.

What all this means in layman's speech is that in about five minutes we were all going to be ass-deep in angels. Angry angels. A Host of them. With Dominion to kill whomever they wanted to, if what the dead angel had said to me was true.

Mostly, that meant me.

"It sounded like a bar fight going on out there," Josh said.

"It was," I said. "Outside, now!"

Josh started to move, thankfully. He led Tiger out to the alley behind the bar. I followed, trying to maintain dodging space between me and Tiger, who had started growling again.

"Tiger, stop," Josh said, sounding uncomfortable. I know he was wondering if letting Tiger at me wasn't a good idea.

"My car is this way. We've got to get out of here before…police arrive."

I mean, it wasn't entirely a lie.

I hurried down the alley toward the street, past a whole mural of gang graffiti—though I noticed a few arcane angelic sigils stuck in there for good measure. You can usually find them on the outsides of buildings marked for some purpose—like murder.

Josh, not even noticing, followed me to my car, Tiger piloting him on. "Are you going to take me to Vivian? How do you know her?"

I stopped and turned to face Josh. Tiger backed up so he was wedged between Josh's knees. He was still growling at me, and I knew we were going to have to work on our relationship some. "When Vivian was eighteen she told you she accidently killed her boyfriend Mitchell," I said, hedging on the bet that Vivian and Josh were close, really close, the way brothers and sisters should be. According to the report I'd read, Josh had taken care of Vivian all the way up until he'd lost his vision. "She still deals with the guilt of that every single day."

Josh paled but I could see that what I had said was true. "You really know Vivian," he finally said.

"Yeah, Josh, and she needs you right now. Badly."

From the corner of my eye, I saw a shimmer of bright lights. I knew what that meant. A door was opening. Through the almost blinding luminescence, I could see tall creature-things emerging. A lot of them. With faintly glowing eyes. Shit. Things had just gone from *bad* to *get the fuck out of Dodge*. Immediately, Tiger began growling again. He didn't like the agents of the Throne any more than I did. Good boy!

"Please get in the car," I begged, running around the front end of the car and jerking open the driver's side. A few seconds later the car rocked as Josh let Tiger in the backseat. Then he jerked the passenger side open and slid inside next to me.

I started the car, hoping Tiger was properly car-trained. I checked my rearview mirror, flinching at the scary, glowy things there, then stomped on the gas and tore down the street. The last things I needed were angels on my ass and a giant dog pissing all over my upholstery.

# | 13 |

ON THE WAY back to Blackwater, I got to know Josh Summers better. He was actually a pretty cool guy. He'd seen all kinds of front-line combat in the Marines. Definitely a fighting man—a man after my own heart.

Some Al-Qaida extremists had driven a truck loaded with explosives into the US Marine Corps headquarters in Afghanistan. It had exploded with the force of twelve thousand pounds of TNT, killing over fifty of Josh's fellow Marines and injuring over a hundred more of them. Josh had been among the injured. The Marines gave Josh a Medal of Valor and sent him home. Vivian took care of him until he could function on his own again. Now it was him, Tiger, and his steel guitar most nights, he said.

It occurred to me that for a guy who'd had his entire life screwed up by religious extremists, he was in pretty good spirits. "How do you deal with something like that?" I mused. "I'd be mad as hell."

"Mad at the guys who blew up the base?" Josh said with genuine interest. "The whole cell died, Nick. There's no one left alive to be mad at."

"I mean, it doesn't seem fair. So fucking useless that something like that should happen at all."

"Oh, I was pissed, believe me. But then I got over it." He dug a small silver cross out of his shirt. It glinted in the lights of the parkway and pretty much guaranteed that we'd never have a date. "He helped me get through it. Him and Vivian."

"Ah."

"You don't believe."

"Let's just say God and I aren't on speaking terms at present."

"You lost someone," he said, and tucked the cross away.

My jaw hurt where I was clenching it. "He lets a lot of shit go on that shouldn't go on."

"Like He should be cleaning up all our messes? I mean, we're not children, Nick."

Were we really having a theological debate in the middle of the Pennsylvania Turnpike? Jesus.

"You're like some kind of country western song," I said as I worked on sticking paper napkins from Dairy Queen up my bleeding nose. I'd meant it as a compliment. "Like something George Jones would sing about."

"How old are you?" he asked. "Everyone listens to Keith Urban now."

"I remember Lynyrd Skynyrd. And hair metal. I have no idea who Keith Urban is."

Josh grinned. "What the hell is my sister doing with an old, cynical fart like you?"

"We have some common interests."

"Not music, obviously. My sister likes pop. Pussycat Dolls, Lady Gaga, that type of thing."

"The chick with the weird hair."

"The chick with the weird hair, yeah."

"And that's why you play Robert Johnson covers."

"Touché." He turned to me then. "You're a salty one. No wonder my sister likes you. She doesn't usually date guys unless they're a *challenge."* He got serious then and turned his head to face the road. "What kind of trouble is she in now?"

I thought about what I could tell him. Not the truth, obviously. I didn't foresee that going over well. So I settled on the facts as the police knew them—and on my suspicions that someone from Vivian's past might be involved.

Josh was quiet a long time. I watched the night-lights of the turnpike flicker over his face through the windshield. In the backseat, Tiger whined.

"Jesus. They gonna convict her?" he finally asked when he had pulled himself together sufficiently.

"Not if I can help it. But Vivian needs you. She wants to see you."

I saw Josh press his lips together. Adopted siblings can be closer than blood relations, mostly because they choose to be close. "Can we pull over at a rest stop? Tiger needs to pee. And so do I."

I knew there were no rest stops on this particular stretch of highway, so I pulled into the first available all-night Kwik Fill. Josh got out and let Tiger pee at the edge of the parking lot. He then got a bright blue doggie apron out of his guitar case and slid it over Tiger's back. The apron had big white letters on it that read *Guide Dog: Please Don't Pet Me – I'm Working*. He then went inside to use the john. I followed him in. The counter girl gave the two of them a disapproving look before spotting the apron.

While Josh was taking care of his business, I collected some sodas from the refrigerated section of the store, then picked up some Halloween Tastykakes. As an afterthought, I also picked up some Beggin' Strips for Tiger. I took my purchases to the counter and yawned while I was paying for them. It occurred to me that I hadn't slept in almost twenty-four hours. I probably looked like shit dragged behind a bus. Thankfully, all the damage the angels had dealt me had been to my belly and ribs under my jacket. My nose had stopped bleeding five miles back. I looked like hell when I thought to check in the security camera above the counter—paler than usual, with dark rings under my eyes like some strung-out meth addict—but not so frightful that the college-age cashier should run off shrieking into the night. I hoped.

She gave me a pitying look as she handed me a new pack of Camels and my change. "Rough night?" she said.

I scratched at my beard. "Rough life. The whole world's going to hell."

"I know what you mean," she said to be friendly. She shook her head and popped her gum. "I wonder when the President is going to turn this country around."

I shrugged and left the store.

\* \* \*

When I got back to the car, I saw Josh was already in the passenger seat, slumped down. He had fallen asleep. Wow. I wished I could drop off that fast.

I got in the driver's side and closed the door, trying not to disturb him. Josh didn't move an inch. I slid the Pepsis into the cup holders and opened a package of Tastykakes. Tiger whined from the back seat. I turned in my seat as I gobbled a Kreepy Kake and regarded him carefully. "So how come you don't like me?"

Tiger growled softly.

"I bought you a treat but you're not going to get it if we can't be friends."

Tiger put his big head down on his big paws and glared at me. He would not bow to bribes.

"You're supposed to be my buddy, like in the *Omen* movies."

Tiger growled.

"I hate those movies too." I finished another Kreepy Kake and took a long swig of Coke to wash it all down. I like to believe that my body metabolizes sugar into magic. It's not likely, but it makes me feel better about loading up on all the cheap carbs all the time. "Especially that kid, Harvey Whatshisname. He wasn't scary at all, and I *know* scary. But I liked Gregory Peck. And Lee Remick was hot."

Tiger had finally lifted his head and was regarding me with something other than plain-faced hostility. That was something. I reached for the Beggin' Strips and offered him one. He carefully sniffed my hand.

"There's nothing I can do about the demon thing, buddy. Sorry."

Tiger took the treat from me, swallowing it down in one gulp. Then he whined.

I gave him another treat, lit a Camel, and started the car. It was a start, at least.

\* \* \*

Josh jerked awake five miles outside Blackwater. Since he moaned and thrashed around in the seat until he was fully awake, I was willing to bet he was reacquainting himself with the day the bomb went off and changed his life forever. I liked him and I hated the people who had done this to him. I wondered how surprised they'd been when their homemade bomb had blown them not into Allah's arms but into my dad's court.

I waited until he'd settled down again. "You want a smoke?" I asked.

"Please." He sounded hoarse, and his face was coated in a sheen of sweat.

I gave him an unlit Camel, then wondered if I'd goofed. Maybe I should have lit it for him? But after a few seconds of fumbling, he'd managed it with the Zippo in his jacket pocket. I probably would have set myself on fire.

"Fuck," he said, leaning back in his seat.

"My thoughts exactly."

"Where are we?"

"Five miles outside Blackwater."

"Can I see Vivian?"

"Visiting hours aren't until ten in the morning in the county lockup."

"What time is it now?"

"Six."

"Fuck," he said again.

"I'll take you to see her later today."

"I'd appreciate that." He sat up in his seat and ran his hand over the dashboard. "This a Dodge?"

"Monaco. 1977."

"The TJ Hooker car."

"Yep."

"Sweet. You're a cop, aren't you?"

I laughed at that. "I was a cop. I'm not anymore." I crushed out my Camel and lit a new one. Another nice thing about the Monaco is it has a huge ashtray.

"So what do you do for a living? Other than chauffeur blind guys and their dogs around?"

"Are you worried about how I'll support your sister?"

"No, just nosy."

"I run an occult shop. I fleece tourists for a living."

Josh nodded. "So you sell bullshit you don't believe in, like politicians and televangelists."

I laughed. "Oh, I believe in it."

He raised his eyebrows at that but didn't say anything. Maybe he figured one debate about God was enough for the night. He didn't know me well enough for us to go at it again. "How'd you come by such a sweet car?" he asked instead.

"It's not a sweet car. It's a piece of shit." I tapped the steering wheel. "I got hit four times in this little lady while working vice down in New York, but she came through for me every time. I totaled the last guy. I can't part with her now."

The greyest rim of morning was just beginning to halo the Lehigh Valley mountains by the time we arrived at the shop. I parked behind the shop and led Josh and Tiger up the back stairs.

The loft was empty. Morgana had left me a handwritten note on the kitchen table, fearful I wouldn't check my cell for messages (which I hadn't, incidentally). I read the note while Josh let Tiger lead him around and familiarize himself with the new surroundings. Morgana said in the note that she was staying the night at Anton's, and that tomorrow—that is to say, today—she and Anton would be going over his friend's book, trying to decipher the meaning behind the angel dolls. She said Anton was very interested in them. And in me. In return for translating the book, Anton hoped I would speak to his coven. About what, I had no idea. I only knew Dark Magic. She would contact me if and when they discovered anything useful.

Since I wasn't opening the shop until noon, I had a few hours to catch up on some much-needed shuteye. I offered the bed to Josh but he insisted on crashing on the sofa instead. He said it was more luxurious than a lot of the places he'd been while touring Philly. Besides, he said, I sounded like I was tired and needed my bed. I thought about pointing out that I had every intention of sleeping in my bed with him, then didn't. Morgana was right. I was probably a pervert.

I yawned for the *nth* time. All the sugar and caffeine in my system had been used up, and the places where I hadn't been able to heal myself were starting to hurt big time. I took a very hot shower, downed six ibuprofens, and crashed hard, although it took me some time to find a comfortable position that didn't aggravate my bruises, of which I had many. I thought about Vivian, which just made me more restless. And horny. She'd likely not find me very sexy now, I thought. From roughly the neck down I looked like the victim of a gangbanging.

Not that I was complaining. I'd taken on two Cherubim and lived. Go, me.

## | 14 |

I WOKE TO a teeth-rattling crash coming from the kitchen. I was fully awake and out of bed with a gun in my hand in approximately two-point-five seconds. I would have moved faster, but I was still sore from the night before, and groggy from all the painkillers.

Tiger growled as I stepped naked into the kitchen, then fell silent. Josh stood at one of the open cupboards, a scattering of tins and cans on the floor surrounding him.

"Sorry," he said, running his hands over the counters. "I think your cupboard is booby trapped. I just opened it and everything fell out."

"I wouldn't know. I don't go in there."

"You don't go in your own cupboards?"

I shrugged, then realized he couldn't see me. "I just keep tea in the canister by the stove. Everything else I order out."

"And you're still alive?"

I grinned. "I'll be right back."

I checked out my bruises in the bathroom mirror while I dressed. All but the worst were yellowing. The magic and the ibuprofen were doing their job. I returned to the kitchen and started hunting for the coffee that Josh needed. Hey, we all have our vices.

"Instant all right?" I asked. I couldn't find anything but an old jar of Folgers Crystals.

Josh shivered. "That'll do, I guess."

"Tell you what. I'll get some real coffee from the Dollar General across the street."

"I don't want you going out of your way."

"Tiger needs food too, right?"

Josh shrugged.

"I'll be right back. Stay put."

I took the gun and my jacket to cover it up, even though it was still unseasonably warm for October. No reason to upset the natives. I didn't think anyone, not even angels, would break into my place with a combination of security spells plus Tiger on the alert.

In the Dollar General, I bought coffee for Josh, a bag of Pedigree for Tiger, and some Honey Buns.

My cashier was talking to the woman in front of me about Vivian. "I hope they give her the chair," she was saying, a hungry sneer on her over-painted face. "But I bet she gets out of it like Casey Anthony did. They'll say there's not enough evidence to convict her, even though there was blood on her when the police brought her in."

"There was blood?"

The cashier nodded with authority. "She had it all over her clothes. She probably killed the little girl too. I wouldn't doubt it."

"You could be right about that," said the woman in front of me as she took her receipt and picked up her purchases. She looked uncomfortable suddenly. "I can't see how two murders could happen in this town and not be related."

"I'm sure you're right."

I made certain to shortchange the cashier.

Josh was appalled when I got back with my purchases and spilled them out on the kitchen table. "You know drinking herbal teas does *not* counterbalance this much sugar in your diet," he said, picking up a squishy Honey Bun. "How much do you weigh?"

"One hundred seventy on a good day," I told him as I looked over the local paper. Behind me, Josh's coffee perked away. The press hadn't yet been let in on Vivian's murder charge. The police were keeping things pretty hush-hush until the prosecuting attorney had a decent First Degree case to present. That wasn't likely to keep tongues from wagging like crazy, though. Everyone in town already believed Vivian was guilty as hell.

"How do you do it? I'm twenty-six and just walking by an open package of Oreos makes me fat."

"Clean living and a pure heart."

Josh snorted. I sat down opposite him at the kitchen table while Tiger nosed into a bowl of dog kibble, scattering a great deal of it across the kitchen floor. Josh reached into his wallet and took out a photograph, sliding it across the table to me. "That's me ten years ago. Sad, isn't it?"

I took the picture and laid it on top of the newspaper.

"I don't know why I keep it," he said. "Sentimental, I guess."

The picture showed three adolescents standing on a dock at the height of summer. Josh was the tall, bony teen in the middle. He was grinning hugely and had his arms around two girls. I immediately recognized the girl on his right. It was a leggy, coltish version of Vivian, her hair tied back. She was wearing a red and white polka-dot bikini. Even at such a young age, there was sex in every inch of her. The girl on Josh's left looked familiar too, though I didn't immediately recognize her. She was chubby and looked chronically unhappy. I thought she might be local. "Who's the girl in the white one-piece?"

"That's Billie, Vivian's best friend at the time."

"Billie..."

Josh thought about that. "Billie Berger."

I glared up at him. "Of the Blackwater Bergers?"

"I think so."

"Rebecca and Thom Berger have an older girl?"

Josh looked at me funny. "Thom Berger does. But Billie's mother's name was Carrie. She died about five years ago in a car wreck, I remember Vivian saying."

"So Rebecca Berger is Thom Berger's second wife?"

"I didn't know he remarried but I guess. Vivian doesn't really talk about them much anymore. She lost touch with Billie a long time ago." He picked at a Honey Bun. "We used to vacation up here when our parents were alive. I guess you can say Vivian and Billie did that whole summer sisters thing, you know?"

I thought about that. I asked Josh about Carrie Berger, but he couldn't remember much, except Vivian trying to contact Billie after she'd learned about her mother's death. By then, though, Billie had moved away from Blackwater and left no forwarding number or address.

I pulled my phone out and Googled Carrie Berger. A local news article stated that she'd been sideswiped by a moving truck one morning on the way to work and wound up in a coma in ICU. It lasted five weeks. At the end of it, she passed on. I then did something I should have done a long time ago and popped Thom Berger's name into the search engine. I found a wedding announcement for Thom Berger and Rebecca Coledale, a nurse from Lehighton, dated only three months after Carrie Berger died of her injuries. Thom certainly hadn't let any grass grow under his feet.

I looked at the wedding picture of Thom and Rebecca Berger but the LCD screen of the cell phone was too small to make out any good details. I flipped through the newspaper until I found a picture of Thom and Rebecca Berger in the back pages, the two of them apparently standing on their front porch and being interviewed by Shelley Preston when the photo had been snapped. Thom was grasping his wife's hand in solidarity. Above the article was the headline BLACKWATER COUPLE PLEADS FOR INFO ON MISSING DAUGHTER. Shelley had made certain the paper had printed a nice big photo with herself almost center frame. Good ol' Shelley. I looked at Josh's photo, then back at the newspaper caption, then Josh's old photo again as something clicked. "Jesus."

"What's wrong?" Josh said, retrieving his cup of coffee.

Tiger stopped slopping kibble all over the kitchen floor and growled at me.

"Can I keep this picture?" I asked Josh. "Just for a little while?"

"Sure. I guess."

While Josh availed himself of my shower, I made a call to an old friend of mine down at the 66th Precinct in Brooklyn. Deputy Inspector Ari Spencer picked up on the third ring. I immediately said, "So, Spencer, are you for hire?"

"Must be smartass Englebrecht," Spencer said.

I grinned. "How'd you guess?"

"The gravelly voice, mostly. You're the only guy I know who sounds possessed," he laughed.

Spencer, Peter, and I had all been new recruits back in the day. Obviously, only Spencer had gone on to live the dream. We passed a few friendly words before I dropped the bomb. "Is there any chance you could run a few names for me? I also have a pic of a potential suspect."

"A suspect? I thought you were out of this game?"

"I'm gumshoeing it," I told Spencer. "This is important."

I heard Spencer fumbling around for a pad and pen. Of all of us, Spencer had been the least organized. I found it pleasantly ironic that he had climbed the ranks so fast. "Go ahead."

I gave Spencer the names of Thom Berger, Billie Berger, and Rebecca Coledale. "Do you have an email? I can send the pic right over."

"Wow, you know how to use the Internet, Englebrecht?"

"I'm evolving," I told him. I used my phone to snap a picture of Josh's photo and then sent it on to Spencer's email. "How long before you can get back to me on this?"

"I don't know, Englebrecht. I have this thing called a *job*, you know."

"Now who's a smartass? Call me as soon as you have something." I smiled. "Please."

I hung up.

Tiger padded over and cocked his head at me. A long thread of drool hung from one corner of his mouth.

"You want another treat?" I asked.

Tiger whined.

I put my hand out. "First you gotta pay the devil his due, buddy. Nothing in life's free."

Tiger moved closer. I petted him on the ears, then gave him another Beggin' Strip.

\* \* \*

I was down in the shop, selling some herbs to Mrs. Bailey when Spencer called me back. He said things were huge. I thanked Mrs. Bailey for her business and closed down the shop for lunch. Then I planted my ass down on the stool behind the counter and got my pad and pen out. "Shoot."

"That one name you gave me, Billie Berger, came back pretty hot. She had some rap, Englebrecht. Possession, prostitution, assault. She finally disappeared about five years ago, presumed dead.

She'd been involved with a lot of bad people over the years, so it's not really a shocker."

"Like?"

There was a pause as Spence looked over what was presumably quite a database. "She was involved in a lot of guru cult-related shit, ran some sites that drained pension money from little old ladies looking to contact the dead, that type of thing. One of her last ports of call before she disappeared was The Order of the Golden Dawn. That's Anton LaVey's group, right?"

"Aleister Crowley, actually."

"And there were a few other groups she'd been associated with over the years but I can't even say some of the names." He spelled them out to me and I wrote them down. About half of them I'd never heard of. That was pretty sad when you think about it. If I was going to be the future ruler of hell, I should probably know my constituents, right?

Nothing suspicious had come back on Thom Berger. Not even a traffic ticket. Damn.

"And Rebecca Coledale?"

"Apparently she's from Lancaster, one of the Amish towns, Elizabethtown to be exact, according to her college records."

"Are there any pictures of Rebecca from back in Elizabethtown?"

"None. She didn't have any pictures taken until she needed a student ID. Now that's odd."

"Not really if she comes from an Amish community. They think pictures are a sign of pride and bringing attention to oneself."

"And you live with these people now?"

I laughed at that. "Anything else on Rebecca Coledale?"

"Nothing. No police records. I guess they raise 'em right in the Amish towns."

"How about the pic?"

"It's a younger Billie Berger. But you knew that, right?"

"I have one more thing for you. Check your email in about two minutes."

I snapped a pic of the caption in the paper of Thom and Rebecca standing together and sent that too onto Spencer's email. I didn't include any part of the article. Then I waited.

About five minutes later, he came back on the line. "So basically you're telling me you found the missing Billie Berger girl and she's all grown up."

"Nope," I said. "*That's* Rebecca Coledale."

\* \* \*

While I drove Josh down to see his sister at the county lockup, I told him what I knew about Billie Berger and Rebecca Coledale.

"You think Billie came back under an assumed name?" he asked.

"Not an assumed name. Rebecca Coledale was a real person from an Old Order Amish colony in Elizabethtown, but I think she's dead now. I even called Elizabethtown and got the community elder. He said they remember Rebecca, but she ran away to Philadelphia in her early teens. She never wrote her family or let them know where she was. Of course, by then she'd been excommunicated so no one really cared."

Josh sat back in his seat and looked very pale. "You think Billie *killed* Rebecca Coledale and took her name?" He sounded appalled.

I nodded as I piloted the ship-like Dodge down the Strip. There was another reason I loved her. She was huge and virtually indestructible. Almost nothing short of an SUV was willing to cut me off. While I maneuvered around all the weekend traffic, I told Josh what I believed: that all of this was tied into Brittany's murder.

Then I asked him what he knew about the Bergers, but it wasn't much. He said Vivian could tell me more about Billie than he could.

The two girls used to play in the woods behind the Berger house during the summer. He only knew that Thom and his first wife Carrie had fought a lot, sometimes in front of the children. Carrie often became hysterical, but he didn't know why. He said Billie ran away from home when she was thirteen years old and no one ever heard from her again.

"Billie and Rebecca were the same age, then," I said. "They may have looked alike too."

"Isn't that kind of hard to do today, with fingerprints and all?" Josh asked.

I shook my head. "Difficult but not impossible. Rebecca Coledale came from a very strict order. They don't take pictures or keep very good birth records in the old orders. Rebecca was a runaway too, and maybe the two of them met up. Maybe they got to be good friends. Then Billie saw an opportunity, a way to become someone different, someone with no rap sheet or record."

I gave Josh a smoke before going on. I thought he might need it.

I told him that Billie likely studied nursing as Rebecca Coledale, and when she was ready, returned just in time to take care of the comatose Carrie Berger, her own mother. I didn't add that it was likely, with the occult connections she had formed down in Philadelphia, that Billie/Rebecca might have even caused the accident that ended her mother's life. There was probably a link there, but I didn't know how deeply I wanted to involve Josh in the supernatural end of things. I liked Josh. A lot. Friends don't let friends drive the supernatural highway. Instead, I said, "Billie may have even killed Carrie Berger. It wouldn't take much to end a coma patient's life, especially if you're a trained nurse."

"Billie put her own mother in the grave and herself in Thom's marriage bed." He shivered, violently. "You know this is freaky even for Blackwater, and I've seen some pretty freaky shit in this town."

"Blackwater was established at a crossroads. It's inclined to freaky shit."

"So back to Billie."

"*That* gets freakier."

"If Billie ran away, why come back? Why do all this elaborate shit?"

"You said the Bergers argued."

"That's putting it mildly."

"Maybe Thom was abusing the girl. Maybe that's why Carrie got hysterical."

"So Billie comes back? She marries her own father? That doesn't make sense. Aren't you supposed to run *away* from abuse?"

I thought about what Vivian had said about Mr. McCarty. "Not everyone does. It's called Stockholm Syndrome. The abused develops such a strong bond with her abuser that she'll do anything to be with him again."

"So how come Thom never noticed he's dicking his own daughter? I mean, that's something you'd realize, wouldn't you?"

"Would you? Her hair's different. She's ten years older. A lot of people in Blackwater look alike." I shrugged. "Or maybe Thom knows and just doesn't give a damn."

"You don't think much of people, do you?" Josh said.

I thought about that. I wondered if he was right.

Josh let me off the hook. "Assuming what you say is true, what about Cassie? Do you think Billie killed her own daughter?"

"Yes," I said.

"Reason being?"

That was the one little thing I still hadn't quite figured out just yet. "The girl was disabled by Tay-Sachs Syndrome. She required almost round-the-clock care from her parents. Maybe Billie was tired of caring for her. Or maybe she was afraid Thom Berger would turn his affections on Cassie in time."

Josh made a face. "Jesus, Nick. If I keep hanging with you I'm going to wind up suspecting everyone of something."

"Everyone's guilty of something."

"Even you?"

"Even me."

"You said Brittany's murder is tied into this." Josh leaned back in his seat and his face went rock hard. "Do you think Billie killed Brittany too?"

"It's a theory," I said, recalling the discussion in the Dollar General between the cashier and her customer. "Billie needed to deflect any possible investigation away from her. What better way than to stage a gruesome small-town murder? It's sensational. It's already pushed the Berger ordeal to the back pages. Another few weeks and no one will even remember Cassie Berger is still missing."

"But why Brittany? Why involve Vivian?"

"Billie knew Vivian as a child. Maybe she kept track of your sister over the years, all that stuff with Mitchell. It's easier to pin a bad crime on someone with a rap sheet and a bad reputation than someone who's squeaky clean."

Josh looked at me then, his face touched with hostility. "Viv doesn't have a bad reputation," he snapped. "She's just had a rough time growing up. My parents didn't make it easy on her, being adopted and all."

Me and my big mouth. "I don't mean she's a bad person, Josh, just that she's been in trouble. I've been in trouble too. It makes a great big target out of you."

He was silent a long moment as he got his temper back under control. I had finally hit his hot button—Vivian. Ironically, that was my hot button too. "Can any of this stuff actually get Vivian off?"

"It can if I can prove that Rebecca's lying about her identity and killed her daughter."

"How do we do that?"

I scratched my chin. "I'm working on that."

Once we arrived at the Bucks County Jail, I saw Josh inside, but stayed in the waiting area and pawed through a beaten copy of *Field and Stream Magazine*. I felt that Josh deserved some private time to talk to his sister. It's what I would have wanted.

I looked around. The walls were painted a depressing shade of high school green and were covered in cheerless yellow posters about spousal abuse. I watched families pass me on their way to visiting incarcerated loved ones. I saw those same loved ones being escorted in or out of rooms, dressed in bright orange jumpsuits. One young punk shambled by, his hands in cuffs and a correctional officer on each arm, but he managed to make me the sign of the horns as he turned his back.

I don't know why some people just look at me and figure I'm *that guy*. I don't look especially evil. At least, I hope not. I glanced up at the security mirror in one corner and picked at my awry hair, which made me look a little like a bargain-basement Jareth wannabe from *Labyrinth*. Jesus. Did that mean the Devil looked like a gay rocker fairy from the 1980s? My dad was going to have a conniption fit.

Twenty minutes later, Josh stepped out with Tiger dressed in his blue apron. He looked strangely blanked of all emotion. "My sis wants to talk to you."

I went inside the visiting room and sat down with the glass division between us. Vivian looked tired, her face unnaturally pale with dark rings under her eyes. I slid my hands through the slot and she took them. She said, "They found evidence of the Cassie kidnapping on my computer at home. Web searches on kidnapping girls, instructions on how to dispose of a body. Ridiculous stuff. None of it's mine." Like her brother, she looked at me blankly, strangely resolved to this. She looked a lot like how I imagined a drowning person looks when they realize they're just floating in the ocean, waiting to die, no rescue in sight. "The state attorney pulled my records, Nick, my rap sheet. Everything. One of the investigators wants to reopen the case on Mitchell. They have the death penalty in Pennsylvania, don't they?"

I grasped her hands, tight. "I'm not going to let anything happen to you."

"I told Josh I'm really glad our parents are gone now. We never got along, but I wouldn't want them seeing me like this."

"We'll get through this," I told her. "I won't let them nail you with this. And the day they release you, we'll go for donuts and coffee."

She smiled, a little. "I appreciate you watching over Josh, Nick. You don't know how much that means to me. Josh, he's..." She shrugged. "He's the only good thing left in my life. The only thing that I haven't screwed up."

We spent the next fifteen minutes talking about Billie Berger, and I wrote down everything that Vivian said. It confirmed everything I'd suspected. Billie had been sexually abused by her father from a very young age, but she'd sworn Vivian to secrecy about it. Vivian, who had already told Billie about Mr. McCarty, had never told Billie's secret to anyone until now. She'd been too afraid that her parents would find out what Mr. McCarty had done to her and blame her for it—but Vivian knew what was going on. Thom Berger regularly pandered to his daughter, which led to the vicious rows and hysterics between him and his wife.

So I knew I was right. I just had to find a way to convince a judge.

At the end of it, Vivian said, "Can I ask you something very personal, Nick?"

I set my pen down. "Of course."

"You're really the son of the Devil?"

I held her eyes. "I'm really the son of the Devil."

"So can you do contracts?"

I shrugged. Kind of yes, no. Maybe. "My dad told me once, but I don't do that kind of thing. I've never done it."

"Would you do it with me?"

"That won't be necessary, Viv…"

"I want you to." She glared at me, her eyes as shiny as polished aquamarines. "Just in the event something goes wrong—Malach, something. I don't want to belong to anyone above or below. I want to belong to you."

I laughed a little nervously. "I don't know if it works that way between daemons, frankly. I mean, we could wind up married or something…"

"Nick, please. I'm asking you. If someone wants to give you their soul, you have to take it. Right?"

"I wouldn't know what to do with it."

She smiled. "You'd keep it safe." She slid her hands under the partition, palms up. "Please."

I thought of a few arguments, then dismissed them. With the Throne vacated, I truly did not know what would happen to Vivian if she died. Probably nothing good. I put my hands on top of hers. She felt cold.

She stared at me with determined, tearless eyes. "What are the words, Nick?"

"There are no words. You just have to want to do it."

"I want to do it. I want you to have my soul, Nick Englebrecht."

"Then it's done," I said. I dug my fingernails into the soft flesh of her left wrist and drew them slowly down. Vivian shuddered but did not move. My fingernails left four shallow scratches diagonally across her wrist, what historians and witch-hunters had called the witches' mark. When it was done, my own left wrist immediately began to burn coolly, but I ignored it.

Vivian admired the marks. She looked at me and she smiled. "Thank you, Old Nick." She leaned toward me as she stood up and kissed the glass partition separating us.

I stayed seated and watched the guards lead her away. Once I was alone, I slid my sleeve back. Four shallow crimson scratches marked my own flesh. I wasn't entirely certain what they meant, but I thought it was possible we had marked each other.

# | 15 |

I WAS ON the way back to the shop when my cell rang. It was Morgana again. "Anton and I deciphered the language in the Book of Shadows, Nick. It was actually written in medieval French."

"What does it say about the dolls?" I prompted.

Josh looked over at me in question but said nothing.

"We had it wrong, Nick. They're not effigies as you would expect, but *wards*."

"Wards to hold something back?"

"It depends on the dolls' orientation, according to the book. If the dolls are hanging up *Blair Witch*-style from trees, for instance, then yes, they're for holding something back. In this case, angels. But if they're lying down..."

"They're there to hold something in place," I finished. I suddenly had a very sickening feeling in the pit of my stomach. Wards were powerful magic, not always white. With a ward, you can call something to you, send it away, keep it out, or hold it in place *ad infinitum*. "Morgana, I'll need you to take the shop this afternoon. And watch Josh. It's vitally important that I return to those woods immediately."

She must have sensed something in my voice, some urgency, because she said, "That's fine. Are you all right?"

"Yes, of course," I said in an utterly false voice.

"Do you need help?"

"You can't help me with this, Morgana," I told her in all honesty. "No one can." *No one mortal.*

I hung up before she could protest.

Josh was still looking at me oddly. "You have a doll collection, Nick?"

"Yes. A big, bad doll collection that nobody wants. Nobody sane, that is."

"I don't understand."

I was sweating and feeling sick. I couldn't think of a single decent lie so I said, instead, "I found some dolls buried in the woods behind the Berger house. They look like angels. I thought they were effigies—voodoo dolls in layman's language. But they're not. They're wards, according to my partner Morgana. Powerful, dark magic used in reverse conjuring—the summoning of angels. They were put there to hold something underground. Something that wants to get loose. I mean to find out what tonight."

There was a long, breathy silence. Then Josh said, "Um. Okay, then."

\* \* \*

After I dropped Josh and Tiger off at the shop and told them to stay put, I drove down to the local Home Depot in Easton, the next big city over, and went hunting for the perfect shovel. I found it myself because of course there was no one around to help. I included a couple of high-powered flashlights, a bottle of Mountain Dew, and some Skittles. I got back to my car as soon as possible with my booty, slightly disgruntled because I had overpaid on a lot of it. I needed smokes, but I didn't have the time to stop at a convenience store. The sun was already dipping below the mountains. Instead, I drove straight out to the Bergers' place.

I parked the car as close to the wooded area and as far away from the actual house as I could get, which put me in a narrow spot near a creek. It was full of brush and scraggly sweetbay magnolias that scratched my paint job, what there was of it. Brush was good. It would hide the car, I thought.

I got out, armed with soda and candy in my pockets, the shovel balanced across my shoulder like an Old West gravedigger, and a battery-powered lantern in one hand, and started hiking through the woods, following almost the exact same path as the last time I'd been here. The journey went faster this time because I knew where I was going. When I reached the ridge, I didn't hesitate; I skidded down the side and ducked into the utter blackness of the hollow, the lantern in my hand my only beacon.

The ground had been recently disturbed. I supposed Billie had been back at some point to replace the angel dolls I had taken. I could imagine what I had done had probably upset her—I had essentially crossed a number of magical barriers that I'd had no business being anywhere near. Sort of the equivalent of a witch's hi-tech security system. It might even have been one of the reasons why she'd set Vivian up. Not only was she the perfect fall guy for Billie's crimes, but she was connected to me. Two birds, one stone. I'm sure Billie was pretty pissed that I'd disturbed her graveyard.

I stood at the edge of the overturned ground, leaning on the shovel, and stared down at the first big plot before me. I was still experiencing that feeling of malice, of *not-right*-ness, and *keep-out*-ness, but now I realized why. There were wards in the ground, not just to keep whatever was beneath it down, but to keep strangers—in particular, magic-wielders like myself—away from the hollow. I had, in my power and ignorance, crossed the wards and disturbed them. I was my father's son; you couldn't keep me out of anything. You could bind me for a short time, as Emily had done, or you could repel me if your faith was strong enough (most people's aren't), but you could not bar my way.

My dad can walk heaven, hell, and earth. He can even go before the Throne. In fact, one of his duties is to drag the sins of the unrepentant before the sinner on their day of judgment. If he wins his argument, he gets to keep the soul and add it to his personal Legion—sort of like a corrupt prosecutor. That means if you're a very bad person, you go to hell when you die and become either his entertainment or his foot soldier. I've heard that neither job is especially pleasant.

I sighed. I knew I was putting off what had to be done. I jabbed the spade into the earth, pushed down on it with my foot, and began to dig. The little box came up fast enough. I shook dirt off it and opened it up. There was a new angel doll inside. I tossed the box and doll aside. At that moment, I detected a soft, muffled moan that made every hair on my body stand at rigid attention, mostly because it seemed to be coming from *beneath* the ground. I stopped to listen. Even though I knew I was alone, I resettled the Tanaka in the waistband of my jeans where it would be faster for me to get at in a pinch. Yes, I left the safety on. Anyone who goes shoving a gun down his pants with the safety off is not badass. He's looking for castration.

I kept digging. As I dug, the moaning grew louder, and I don't mean pleasant moaning, or moaning like in some cheap-ass horror flick. I mean the kind of sick, pain-filled moaning that creeps along your subconscious, sticks a finger in, and wiggles it around a lot. By the time I hit the anticipated second big box under the first little box, my stomach was in knots and I felt like throwing up all over myself. My sense of pity and revulsion had been kicked into overdrive and I hadn't even fully uncovered the casket yet.

I stopped digging and hunkered down in front of what looked like an old cedar chest, the kind you can buy around here from any antique store. The terrible, heartfelt moaning was coming from inside the box. I had one of those bad moments when I really wanted God to come help me with this because I didn't know if I was strong enough to handle it on my own. Then I remembered that He'd retired—apparently without an heir or replacement—and I was on my own. C'est la vie.

I reached out and pushed dirt off the top of the box. I found some latches along the sides, not locked, and I unclasped them. I thought to myself, I really fucking don't want to do this. Then I reminded myself that nobody else wanted to do it either, but that I was probably the only one capable of it. The only one with the power. Feeling sick to the point of passing out, where darkness was seeping into the corners of my eyes, I dug my fingers into the seam of the lid and pulled it open.

The box had been buried a long time, years, maybe decades. The top virtually disintegrated in my hands. Inside, an angel stared up at me. I knew it was an angel from the way it felt. I couldn't tell by its appearance. It was mottled blue-black in appearance. Its limbs had been surgically removed, along with its lower jaw. The rest was skeleton covered in that purplish, parasite-infected skin. The left side of its heaving breast had been carved away, allowing a lively nest of yellow maggots to feed upon its eternal flesh. Its pale blue eyes were open and very clear. It saw me. It was aware. The smell it gave off was like roadkill mixed with burning sugar.

I got up, turned away, and vomited Mountain Dew and Skittles all over the forest floor and over my own boots. Then I got down on my hands and knees and vomited again, out of my mouth and my nose. That was likely tea and Honey Buns. My stomach cramped up as it searched for more; it was really reaching now. I put my face against leaf litter and just waited until my heart slowed down, my pulse resumed a normal rhythm and my stomach stopped spasming. I told myself I could do this, then I said no fucking way, then I told myself to get my shit together.

"Hell," I said.

Breathing deeply, I pushed myself up and sat back on my haunches. That put me at eye level with a pair of long crossed legs clad in Yves Saint Laurent blue pinstripe, year-round wool trousers. I felt a lurching panic in my chest that I should be taken so unaware, at a point of vulnerability, then I realized who the slacks and the painfully expensive snakeskin Prada loafers belonged to. I raised my eyes and saw the matching blazer and the pressed white polo shirt opened casually at the throat. My dad has this thing about dressing like Tony Soprano. Go figure. He was sitting on a low-hanging pine branch, smoking a Dunhill luxury cigarette and watching me with a combination of sympathy, interest, and contempt. I think mostly contempt.

The pine tree was mostly green, but the branch he sat on had already turned a mottle black color as if it had tree leprosy. I knew that in a matter of days the whole tree would be dead.

"What are you doing here?" I asked as I struggled into a more dignified kneeling position on the ground at his feet.

The Devil smiled at me pleasantly. "I always drop by when you're in trouble, Nicky, you know that."

# | 16 |

MY DAD LOOKS like me, only worse. Fey. Angelic.

Forget the horror movies you've seen. I've never actually met a demon that was ugly. I mean, what's the point? If it was ugly, you'd have nothing to do with it, right? Not to mention that would seriously screw with its ego, and if it's one thing demons have, it's ego.

My Grandpa's signature sin was beauty and pride. I met him once, and he's actually a pretty cool guy, believe it or not, very laid back. He passed that on down to my dad and me. My dad's sin, though, was war and pestilence, hence all the trouble since around the Twelfth Century. But because sins are accumulative in the Lucifer line, my dad is beautiful, proud, high-strung, a warmonger, and a huge pain in the ass. I mean, it's like meeting a big-name Hollywood actor—awesome for about the first half hour. After that, you just want to punch him in the mouth to get him to shut up about himself.

My dad uncrossed his long legs and leaned forward, offering me a handkerchief with a helpful smile so I could wipe my mouth. I pushed his arm away and climbed unsteadily to my feet, wiping my mouth on the sleeve of my jacket instead.

He looked disappointed. "'Folly is bound up in the heart of a child, but the rod of discipline drives it far from him,'" he quoted.

"Fuck you," I said. "What would you know about disciplining a child?"

"You're angry."

Count on my dad to point out the obvious.

I turned and leaned on the shovel stuck in the earth, trying to figure out what I was going to do about the angel in the box. Maybe if I ignored him, my dad would go away. Then I could think straight.

My dad hates being ignored. "The Throne is empty," he said.

I turned on him. "I *knew* you wouldn't be here unless you wanted something. What is it now?"

"I thought you might want to know our great enemy has departed the administrative office."

"I know."

"The Cherubim," my dad said, smirking around his smoke. "You did a good job on those two chumps. The first one's still entertaining me."

"Why is the Throne empty?" I asked.

"So *now* you want me to tell you."

"You're going to tell me anyway."

My dad shrugged and leaned back against the tree. The tree developed more tree-leprosy. "He stepped down. I guess He was sick of all the bullshit. Can't say I really blame Him. I certainly wouldn't want His job. In any event, Gabe and Mike are standing in for now."

"Lovely," I said. "So that's the reason for the Dominion over everyone."

"And the reason you need to be aware of all this. Gabe declared open season on all daemons, and about half the holy Host are behind him. The other half is undecided at this time."

That made sense, I guess. If the Throne was empty, that meant the angels effectively had free will to make up their own minds who they wanted to follow, if anyone. I wondered how they were taking that. Not well, likely. That was a little like a bird born and raised in a cage, then set free one day. I was willing to bet about half of the holy Host were on the verge of having a nervous breakdown.

"Naturally, you're at the top of their to-do list," my dad informed me. He picked invisible lint off his jacket. "Hence the reason I'm here. I want you to come home, Nicky."

"Excuse me?"

He looked up at me, his amazingly blue eyes simmering under his arched brows, then reached up and straightened my jacket for me. "I want you to come home where I can keep an eye on you, protect you."

I laughed in his face. "You must be fucking kidding me. You haven't given a shit about me in forty years and *now* you want to protect me?" I pulled my jacket out of his hold. I stepped back. I could barely keep the disdain from dripping out of my mouth. "I hate to break this to you, old man, but I can take care of myself just fine. I don't need *you*."

"You're so much like your grandfather, Nicky, do you know that? Impetuous. Rebellious." His hand moved faster than I thought humanely possible. He wrapped it around my left hand, where the scars still burned. That made them hurt. A lot. He jerked me closer. "But you're not prepared for this. You're not trained to handle legions of angels operating under their own free will. No one saw this coming."

"And yet, I'll manage. As always." I tried to shake his hold off. I couldn't. "I can handle angels. I trashed two Cherubim just yesterday. Remember?"

"There's more than angels to worry about now."

"Like?"

"Like the Arcana."

I shook my head. That was one of the names that Spencer had given me. "Tarot?"

"Not Tarot. They're an ancient order of angel-eaters. They date back to the Crusades." He let go of my hand. "In fact, they're likely the ones who killed your little friend Peter."

Well, that got my attention, and he well knew it. "What do you mean? Why would anyone want to harm Peter?"

My dad stared at me, the cigarette clenched in his eternally white teeth. I noticed that it never seemed to get any smaller, unlike my Camels. I thought that was a neat trick. "The Arcana seek power, as so many cults do, but not for the reasons you think. They don't consider themselves evil. If anything, they want to save humankind from itself. And as you already know, zealotry can be devastating." He took a deep breath and let it out. The smoke that came out of his mouth was slightly greenish. "Their prophets told of this day, Nick. The day when the Throne would be abandoned, though no one believed it, including myself. As a result, the cult has been extremely vigilant for over four thousand years. They know the angels serve God in two capacities, as servants *and* as food, and they believe that if one among their number can absorb enough of the angels' flesh and power, they can ascend to the Throne."

I looked at him a long, hard moment. "Ascend as in *be* God?"

"Correct."

"By eating the angels?"

"Exactly."

I stopped to absorb that. It made me wonder if that wasn't part of the motivation behind my grandfather's rebellion in the first place. I knew *I* wouldn't want to be anyone's lunch, even God's. I looked at my dad a little sideways. "Angels are food?"

"Sometimes. Yes."

"God eats his own angels?"

"If His power must be increased, then yes. He consumed legions before creating the world we know today." His hand loosened on my wrist somewhat. "It is no different than drone bees sacrificing themselves to the betterment of a hive, or worker ants dying for their queen. In the end, all of nature mimics its Creator, Nick."

I swallowed. "But why would this Arcana kill Peter? He had no power. He was just a flatfoot from Bensonhurst. He wasn't a daemon. He wasn't even a witch."

"You share your power with mortals, Nick. That can be very attractive to the wrong type of people. If the Arcana cannot have the whole, they will take the part."

I didn't understand this at all. "Do they know about me?"

Dad waved that away as if it was merely bothersome to him. "They've been watching you since the day you were born, Nick. They know who you are. I'm sure the only reason they haven't targeted your Morgana yet is because she has her own power and her spirit guides to protect her." He looked at me gravely in a way I had never seen before. If I didn't know any better, I would have said he was concerned for me. Yeah, I knew better. Dad was only concerned about his investment. "It wasn't random that they should have chosen Peter. They knew what your relationship with him was, and it attracted them."

I laughed bitterly at that. "Well, then, they were wrong! I never had sexual relations with Peter. He never shared in my power." I swallowed again, hard. It felt like a walnut was stuck in my throat. "They didn't let him live long enough for that to happen."

He shrugged. "Ultimately, the Arcana are only human, Nick. They make mistakes."

I stared at him in shock and horror. A kind of electric rage ripped through my body in that moment and the wind picked up substantially, lashing the trees around us. I felt like hitting my dad over and over even though I knew it wasn't his fault. I wanted to pummel him until he was broken and bruised and his beautiful suit was in tatters. I couldn't believe what he was saying, or the flippant way he was saying it. "So that's it? They fucked up and Peter died because he knew me? *He died for no reason?*"

He glared at me. "I wouldn't say for no reason, Nicky. After all, you got a chance to see what they're capable of."

"I don't give a shit what they're capable of!" I raged at him.

"You should. I put a tremendous amount of power into you. If they catch you...consume your flesh..." He shook his head. "Nick, they could conquer this world. They could conquer a *thousand* worlds. Do you understand what I'm telling you?"

"And you just care *so* much about this world that you mean to save it."

"I care about *balance*. It's what I do." He looked so peeved. Good. "Without me, there is no free will in this whole world. Do you understand that?" He lowered his voice. "And I care about *you*. You're an idiot and I worry about you constantly, Nicky. So does your mother."

The trees settled down as I really looked at him. I could hardly believe what he was telling me. "Mom's alive?"

His brows arched in exasperation. "Yes, of course. Did you think she was not?"

"How am I supposed to know?" I yelled at him, gesturing wildly. "You took her away!"

The wind picked up again, this time fiercer than ever. My dad glanced up at the roiling black clouds forming a massive funnel cloud far overhead. Debris suddenly raked past us, kicked up by the storm. Something like admiration flickered in his eyes. He smiled in the seconds before the wind ripped him from his perch and flung him hundreds of feet into the air. I looked on in surprise...and vague horror. I had never done such a thing in my life. I did not even know how I had done it, or how I could undo it.

When my dad reached the thrashing treetops, he halted his own momentum and spread his wings. An archangel, he had eight of them, all of a purest, blinding, feathery white armored in steel and gold. The moment he unfurled them, the night sky lit up like noontime. They formed two massive blinding satellites that made me cringe and turn away as he reversed his trajectory and rocketed through the impromptu storm I had kicked up.

In seconds, he was standing in front of me once more, untouched by my rage. He was smirking. I lunged at him. I punched him in the mouth as his enormous blinding wings beat about me. I clawed at his face, but it was like trying to harm a statue. There was nothing there to hurt, just all burning cold stone. He pushed me down and I landed hard on my ass, staring up at him, ashamed of the way I was acting, the way I wanted to sob like some little kid told there would be no Christmas, no presents, no parents.

My dad dissolved his wings. The forest immediately went from noontime to midnight. He snorted and used his handkerchief to staunch the flow of blue blood trickling over his lips from the broken nose I'd dealt him. "That's a good left hook you have there, son. Maybe anger is your signature sin." He did not sound entirely displeased by the idea.

I didn't answer. The storm had died down, leaving the ground wet and covered in debris. I was sitting in mud, I realized, and my ass was wet and cold. *I* was wet and cold. And tired. And done. My dad dropped down beside me in a lotus position. His suit, though slightly creased, was still immaculate, even in the mud. It wasn't fair. "Feel better?" he asked.

"No," I answered. I covered my face with my trembling hands and wept. I couldn't remember the last time I'd wept. I think it had been in one of my many foster homes. "Go away."

"I'll wait until you're done sniveling."

"Fuck you. Go to hell."

"I don't think that's such a good idea, Nicky." He dropped his handkerchief in my lap. "This is so much bigger than you can handle. And though you have the power, you don't have the training. You can't control the Arcana, Nicky. Hell, you can't even control yourself. I want you to come home."

"No." I scooted back away from him.

He lit a new cigarette and took a long drag, painting the filter of his high-end smoke with his blue blood. He eyed me wisely.

"You're my son, Nick, I hope you realize that." He patted my leg. "You are going to come home one day and you are going to take over the family business. It's what you were created for, and it's going to happen sooner or later. This is non-negotiable, Nicky. You can't run from this."

"Maybe," I said, rubbing my eyes and snotty nose. "But not now. Not yet. I need time." I swallowed hard. "I'm not ready."

He stood up, brushing imaginary debris off his slacks. He looked, if not pleased, then at least resigned. Probably he knew if he tried to drag me to hell, I'd punch him in the nose again and ruin his beautiful suit. "It's a good thing I sent you a partner, then. Things are going to get pretty rough for you from here on out, just so you know."

I opened my mouth, closed it. "What partner?"

He didn't answer, which was pretty typical of my dad. He's like a Chinese proverbial question that answers its own question, but doesn't answer anything at all. "A little fatherly advice, son: it gets worse the longer you stay here among the humans. It makes it harder to do what needs doing when you finally go home. You can become very attached to these…creatures, believe me."

I was trembling too much to get to my feet so I just sat there, staring up at my old man. I still hated him, but I knew he was probably right. "What happened to Peter?"

Dad looked interested.

"Is Peter with you?" I said, dreading the answer.

He considered that. "Well, that's for you to find out one day, isn't it?" He looked over at the big hole in the ground that I had dug. "What are you going to do about Jack in the Box there?"

I knew I would get no more answers from him. The bastard. I took a deep breath to steady myself. "Billie did this. She's part of the Arcana, right?"

"Yes."

"So if I free the angels, destroy their second hearts, then her power will be undermined. Diminished."

"Maybe." He gave me a shrewd look. "But I think you just want to kill those angels."

I sat there huddling, feeling cold and miserable and alone. I remembered huddling a lot in big cold orphanages and juvie halls all over Bensonhurst and Brighton Beach. Back then, I used to dream about who my father might be. I used to pretend he was a famous astronaut or a fireman, a secret agent or someone running from the mafia. I used to believe that he would come for me one day and tell me everything was all right, that he was safe, that he could take care of me now. But he never came. Not until I was *useful* to him.

"They're soldiers," I told him. "I don't want them to suffer like this. I wouldn't want *anyone* to suffer like this. It isn't fair."

My dad smirked in a knowing way, raised his hand, and opened a door in the thin mountain air. I couldn't see much beyond a shadowy, ever-shifting darkness, but I could hear things—base things, suffering things, sexual things—things that human beings have no business hearing. "You know, I think you're right, Nicky. You're *not* ready...but you will be soon." Still smiling, he reached into his breast pocket and tossed me his pack of Dunhills. "You're a prince. Get some better cigarettes, will you?"

He disappeared into the void.

# | 17 |

I LIT A Dunhill and smoked it down before approaching the hole in the ground again. By then, night had turned the woods into a velvety blackness full of swarming things. I turned the flashlights on and aimed them at the hole in the ground. I thought maybe I had imagined everything, but the angel was still there, still desiccated and helpless, staring up at me with pleading blue eyes. Its tongue moved like a dirty worm in its mouth, but it had no jaw to formulate any words. I wondered what it would say to me if it could speak. My horror had been replaced with a terrible, abiding sadness.

"I'm really sorry, friend," I told it. I wondered, absently and rather uselessly, if it was a Seraph or a Cherub, not that such a thing mattered much now, I supposed. "I know you probably don't think much of me, but I'd like to be a friend to you tonight. I'd like to help you along to…wherever you guys go back to."

I reached into my boot and pulled loose my athame. It had been a gift from Morgana. It was made entirely of silver with glyphs cut into the blade on both sides. My athame isn't magical—at least, no more than I am. It has no sordid history that I'm aware of. It isn't blessed or cursed. It's just a knife I use in rituals, when I feel the need to initiate them. Tonight, though, I was going to do things with it that good witches never do.

I leaned over the angel and placed my hand on its sunken, skeletal chest. I positioned the blade of the knife over its belly, where its holy second heart still beat. "Sorry," I told it and cut deftly down, very fast. The knife sliced right through the body like it was made of papier-mâché. Within seconds I had the cavity open and I could see all the angel's alien organs pulsing like jellied jewels inside of it. Had I still been horrified, I wouldn't have been able to do it. But I was tired. I kept thinking about my father, what he'd said about my inescapable fate, how my life was not my own. I just wanted this to end.

I grasped the shining, warm, fluttering heart in my hand like a little bird and sliced it loose. The heart began to disintegrate almost before I had it out of the cavity of the angel's chest. The pale eyes fluttered in the once-beautiful, demolished face. The rest of the angel followed, sweetening with decay and then crystallizing so quickly I held nothing but a handful of shining white ash within seconds.

Looking over the ground, I realized I had five more plots to go. I felt numbed, outraged, and terrified all at once. It gave me energy, if nothing else. I climbed to my feet, picked up the shovel, and began to dig.

I learned many things about Billie as I uncovered each of her victims. She generally worked on the extremities first, but sometimes it was specific organs she wanted, the eyes or the tongue, for instance. Sometimes arms and legs were severed and then stacked neatly alongside the angel for later consumption. It was obvious she visited the angel graveyard frequently, that she was trying to extend the life of the creatures she had captured, farm them for as much meat and power as she could, sort of like her own little herd of magical cattle. There was an evil genius at play in all she did. Some of the angels could speak. Most had nothing to say to me. Most looked grateful or simply relieved. I apologized to each one. I cut into each shrunken chest, cut away each frantic, shining white jelly heart, waited until each angel had gone to absolute dust before I moved on to the next. I was efficient, methodical, and, above all, precise.

My formerly un-magical athame steadily grew hotter in my hands the more I used it to help the angels move on. I was either blessing it or cursing it with the work I was doing. In the end, I found I had to wrap my dad's handkerchief around the hilt just to do the work that needed to be done. I didn't know if what I was doing was good or bad. I just knew it had to be done.

It seemed to take all night, and by the end of it, I was covered in dirt, sweat, and nightmares. I had thrown up twice more in the course of the night's activities, yet I counted that a small victory. It meant I hadn't turned into the cold-hearted bastard that was my father.

I had done all I could for now. I had stolen away Billie's power, and any power she had absorbed would likely not be enough to do anything spectacular.

My cell phone rang, though the number on the LCD display was unfamiliar to me. "Englebrecht," I said, sounding tired and shaken.

There was a pause. Then Morgana's voice said clearly over the line, "Nick...help me..."

The phone went dead in my ear. I looked at it.

I roared. And then I pulverized it against the nearest tree.

\* \* \*

I raced out of the hollow of trees, shining one of the flashlights as I went along. I was scrambling up the ridge when something hissed out of the trees. I immediately turned sideways to make myself a smaller target, but I wasn't fast enough, and in the near perfect dark I couldn't orient myself or determine where the attack was coming from. A knife suddenly appeared in my left shoulder, spun me around, and then I was skidding and falling down the ridge, bumping over rocks and snagging my clothes on sharp branches. I grunted and landed hard on my back in the creek at the base of the ridge.

I gasped, thrashing in the cold water. I sat up and the pain in my shoulder was immediate and intense, like someone was jabbing a hot coal into my wound. I scrabbled at the hilt of the knife, trying to pull it out, but when my hand encountered it, I screamed compulsively. I thought it must be magical, likely an athame designed specifically to hurt angels, which demons and daemons are, when you got right down to it. I let it go. I scrabbled around in the dirt, but my flashlight had bounced away when I landed in the creek and was busily illuminating a ragged pear tree in all its end-of-season glory, a halo of night insects buzzing through the light. That was worth fuck-all to me.

I grunted as I tried to find purchase through all the blinding, crippling pain. I had to get up the ridge and to my car. I had to get home, had to save Morgana. I'd sooner be dead and damned than let what happened to Peter happen to her, or to Josh…

Ahead, I could hear the faint swish of dried leaves as someone descended the ridge with a lot more grace than I had. Someone laughed, not an evil sound but a joyous one. It was the sound of someone very close to victory.

I had a decision to make in that moment. I could go for the light or the gun. Visions of Peter flickered through my brain like a horror movie that wouldn't let go. I decided that faced with an angel-eater out to get me, I'd rather be armed with a handgun than a flashlight. I turned, wriggling the huge handgun out of my jeans with my right hand—my left was like a big chunk of lifeless meat attached to me—and took blind aim from my position on the ground.

The first muzzle flash illuminated the terrible, holy visage of Billie descending, dressed in a white ceremonial robe—skin glowing like a ghost, pale hair writhing. She fell upon me seconds later, her face twisted in lust and determination. The second blast made her scream and fall back. It also made me grin in devilish delight.

I had hit her!

Seconds later, I heard the scuffle of feet as Billie regained her balance. A strange bioluminescence seemed to fill the black forest with its ghostlight. It took the form of a woman—a winged woman. Four wings, faintly glowing. It illuminated the gunshot I had put in her shoulder—a burning black hole as big as my fist that was even now beginning to close up.

"Morgana..." I said, almost screaming with the burning pain in my own shoulder—a shoulder that wasn't healing nearly fast enough, certainly not like Billie's wound. "What did you do?"

"Nothing," Billie said in exactly Morgana's throaty voice. "Just some glamour." She pulled out a cell phone and tossed it on the ground between us. "You are so easy, Little Horn...and you call yourself a *witch*." Billie spread her wings and they pulsed with a light similar to the full moon, a light that made me flinch

I realized, belatedly and with some terror, that I was an injured daemon lying on the ground in the dark with what appeared to be a soldier angel charging me. I tried to summon a shield, a door...but my mind was a jumbled mess of fear and pain. The athame in my shoulder ached and pulsed like someone was thrusting a hot knife in and out, so distracting that all I could do was concentrate on escape. With a grunt, I pushed myself unsteadily to my feet, determined to duck into the hollow again in an effort to conceal myself amidst the trees, but the moment I was up, the whole world began to sway dangerously and my legs buckled and I collapsed like a wounded water buffalo amidst the weeds. The athame seemed to be sucking all the strength right out of my limbs. Christ, I really hated angel magic. With my strength ebbing, I tried to raise the gun, my last defense, but no sooner was my arm up, Billie was upon me, her weight bearing me to earth.

"Englebrecht," she said sweetly. "Angel-breaker."

She bit into my wounded left arm and I screamed. And screamed.

\* \* \*

The pain was well nigh orgasmic, and not in a good way. Each bite of Billie's teeth seemed to drag the pain up from my very spine. I screamed as Billie went about the process of eating me alive.

She stopped only long enough to say, silkily, in my ear, "Such power, Dark Prince. And in forty years, you have not so much as scratched the surface of it. You have squandered your father's gift to you." Her voice was husky and stilted, like she was on the edge of coming right then and there.

I arched my back and gagged as she resumed biting into my forearm, right into my wound to get at my ragged, raw flesh and blood. Her gnawing teeth made me writhe like I was conducting an electric current. I kicked at the ground with my heels but I couldn't escape the pain. "Fuck you, bitch." My right hand flailed, coming down hard on something familiar lying in the weeds beside me.

"Shh," she said, stroking my hair. "Be still, daemon, and serve." Her hand moved to my chest, then farther down, and she started pawing at my cock through my jeans. I stayed soft. That part of me had decided it was going to have no part of this insanity, thank you very much. Billie leaned close, her bloodied lips inches from my ear. "You shouldn't have disturbed my garden. Now you'll have to replace it. I need your power. With you, Little Horn, I can Ascend." She bent down and kissed me on the lips. Her cold, sugary-sweet tongue curled inside my mouth.

That's when my hand closed around the grip of the gun lying on the ground. I brought it up and around, hard, connecting with the side of Billie's head. Billie grunted and rolled off me.

I'm left-handed, though you've probably guessed that already. Still, I can shoot with my right in a pinch. My instructor in the Academy taught us to shoot with both hands. I'm not a crack shot, but at close range, that hardly matters. My left arm was numb and virtually useless. I rolled over and brought my right arm around, shooting blind in the direction where Billie had fallen. I saw a flicker of glowing whiteness. I tried to track it. I heard the report of the shot echo through the trees, saw the muzzle flash, heard sleeping birds and small animals screech awake, but otherwise it brought no response.

"Hell," I breathed hoarsely as I struggled to my feet and stumbled around like a drunkard, bleeding all over the ground from my seeping bite wound. It hurt, but now I was mad as hell. Mad is good. It motivated me. I had a madwoman on the loose imbued with the power of the Devil who wanted to be God. Fuck. Could my night get any worse?

Apparently so. Before me, a door *shooshed* up. I saw shifting darkness and colors that just don't exist on planet Earth. Oh fun. Company from the other side. Problem was, I didn't know *which* side. The doors looked all the same to me, at least until I saw the denizens.

I'd just managed to get my equilibrium and was weaving dangerously when a massive pair of patent-leather-gloved hands caught me by the shoulders and steadied me. A hand grasped the athame in my shoulder and jerked it loose without warning. That made me scream like a little schoolgirl as blood and something black and rotten poured out of my wound.

First, I felt pain...then gratitude that a big biker-type dude from the other side had materialized out of nowhere to help me stand up and get that cursed, angel-eating athame out of my flesh. I was about to say, "Hey, thanks," when I realized who that big biker-type dude was.

A booming, unnatural basso said, "Nicky..." with a giant smile in his voice.

"Malach. Nice seeing you here," I croaked. "You're just in time. How are you?"

Malach punched me in the face.

# | 18 |

ATTACKED BY SUPERNATURAL forces...check.

Assault and battery by a magical artifact...check.

Complete and utter loss of all dignity...check.

I figured I was batting zero tonight. I sat shirtless against a tree, smoking the last of my dad's fancy cigarettes and working on binding the giant bite wound in my left arm with strips of my shirt. The pain nauseated me and I kept clutching the wound with my right hand, but my healing mojo was working slow as hell tonight. It was like the athame had sucked the magic right out of my body.

"Why are you taking so long?" Malach asked, pacing back and forth in front of me. He held the giant gold angel gun in both hands as he walked a few paces, stopped to eye the woods, then started walking again in the opposite direction. I had the feeling the gun was the equivalent of his security blanket.

"I'm sorry I'm holding you up, friend," I said, my voice coming muffled and acidic out of my swollen mouth. I tasted blood and at least four of my teeth felt dangerously loose when I probed them with my tongue. Malach had a hell of a right swing, and I don't even think he was putting all he could behind it. "I do just happen to be half human, you know."

"Hurry up."

"Or what? You're going to hit me again? Drag me through the woods?"

He turned and eyed me with his cold blue mechanical eyes. "There's a thought."

I met his gaze unflinchingly. You can call me brave or stupid, I don't care. After all the shit I'd been through tonight, I was *not* going to cower under Malach's tough guy persona. "Why don't you just shoot me already? That's what you're here for, aren't you?" I indicated the woods. "We're not on holy ground now."

"I'm not here to shoot you, Nick. I'm here for the Arcana."

That surprised me. "I thought you were hunting daemons?"

"The Arcana takes precedent over daemons. They are far more dangerous."

"Sure, and that's why you've been following Vivian around for the past three days?"

"I was not hunting your Whore of Babylon because she is a daemon, Nick. I was hunting her because she knew Billie Berger. I thought she might be part of the Arcana."

Well, that surprised me. I thought about busting Malach up for the Whore of Babylon comment, but he'd probably just punch me in the mouth again.

"She's not," I said defensively. "Whatever else Vivian is, she is *not* part of them."

"Yes, Nick," he answered. "I know."

I don't know why, but it made me want to cry with insane joy that Malach called me *Nick*. Malach *always* called me Nick. No stupid names or nicknames, no vainglorious epithets. To Malach I was just *Nick*. It was so goddamn…*normal*.

"Can you get up?" he asked.

"Why? You'll just hit me again."

Malach rolled his eyes. "I am not here to hit you, Nick. I told you. I am here to hunt the Arcana." He paused and seemed to consider that. "And I need your help." He sounded embarrassed by his admission.

I shook my head. "I thought you were here to drag me before the Throne."

"There is no one on the Throne to drag you to," he said. He sounded sad about that. He played with his big gun. He liked his big gun. I'm sure there was something very Freudian about that.

On a hunch, I said, "You're one of the angels who's undecided, aren't you?"

He shrugged one shoulder, the way some guys do, creaking a lot in his dusty black leather. "I do not like the new management."

"I thought you took your orders directly from Gabe?"

His eyes flared. It wasn't something you ever wanted to see directed at you, believe me. "I take my orders from my Lord."

"So why hunt the Arcana?"

"I do not want a human being to Ascend to the Throne. Especially *them*."

The pain in my arm was finally lessening, though I wished I had some ibuprofen or something. I really needed to carry that around with me along with my candy fetish. Mental note on that. Especially considering the amount of people who wanted to knock the shit out of me of lately.

The wrist of my left hand was burning. I looked at it and was surprised by how irritated the witch marks looked. There was no doubt in my mind that Vivian had marked me in return, and the sight of the shallow scratches gave me an idea. We had learned that Vivian could heal through sex. I wondered if I had a permanent conduit to that power…that power that existed outside of me but inside *her*. I pressed the marks to my wounded shoulder and felt warmth infuse the wound. The pain began to drain away.

I decided to give standing a try. I was halfway up the tree when the whole forest started to sway. I leaned back against the trunk and closed my eyes. I was sweating and still feeling sick to my stomach.

"What is wrong with you?"

"I think that athame poisoned me." I clutched my fist closed until the force of it made my wrist marks bleed. Spitting away the cigarette, I brought the blood to my lips, trying to force Vivian's healing power into my body. Malach watched me with interest. "Don't let that bitch put one of those knives in you," I told him after a few moments of licking up my own blood like a second-rate vampire. "If it hurts this much and I'm only half angel, it'll tear the shit out of you."

"Thank you. I will remember that."

The sky was lightening and I could see Malach better. He looked big and badass as usual, like a bounty hunter misplaced from somewhere in the southwest, the deserts of Arizona, maybe. But he also looked a little lost. A little...not Malach. "Why are you doing this?" I asked.

"Doing what?"

"Being nice to me. Not shooting me."

"I told you. I need your help with the Arcana." He smiled then, a little. "Maybe I'll shoot you later."

"You sound like the Terminator with those lines, you know? *Come with me if you want to live.*"

Malach stared blankly at me. Mostly, he did not get my jokes.

My shoulder was feeling better, not mended, but better. Manageable. I slipped the jacket over my bare shoulders, grimacing a little, then pushed myself off from the tree. The woods, already filling with moody grey morning light, still swayed a little, like I was standing on a giant cosmic pendulum, but I decided I could deal.

When you have a whole world to save from a nearly omnipotent bad guy, you can't let a little angel magic get you down. I checked the Tanaka, noting I had plenty of munitions left. "Rock and roll," I said to Malach. "Let's go."

\* \* \*

We started hiking toward the Berger house together. Along the way I said, "You know, I make a better ally than an enemy."

"You are the son of the Lord of the Pit."

"Come on. I'm not *that* bad."

He glared at me.

"Just because I smoke and like sex does *not* make me a bad person. Some would even call me normal."

He glared at me.

I reached into my pocket and found a half-full bag of Skittles. My day was looking up. "You want one?" I asked, offering him the bag.

Malach ignored me. His loss.

"So why'd you punch me if you were here to get my help?" I asked through a mouthful of candies. They tasted funny in my swollen, metallic mouth.

Malach shrugged. "I just always wanted to punch you."

\* \* \*

"There's still one thing I'd like to know," I said when the Berger house came into view a half mile off. "God does have a Son. Why doesn't *He* ascend the Throne?" I had been giving this a lot of thought as we ambled along. Well, Malach ambled. I sort of limped like a lame horse. Malach didn't talk much, so I had had to amuse myself by going over all this in my head.

"The God on the Throne *was* the Son," Malach told me simply.

"So the God line works much the same way as the Lucifer line?"

Malach nodded once. "His Son did not come to Earth to save the humans. He came here to understand them so He would be a better God when it came His turn to take the Throne."

"How's that working out for you guys?"

Malach glared at me.

I popped more candies into my mouth and tasted the rainbow. "And the whole point of the crucifixion, then?"

"There was no point to the crucifixion, except that people can be cruel and insipid."

"Wow, and they say I'm cynical."

Malach looked annoyed, not that that was anything new. "God does not say He will save the humans. He says the humans will save themselves."

"So what's changed then?"

"His Son has lost faith in mankind," Malach said. He bowed his head as if this greatly saddened him, though his expression didn't change at all. Angels: they wrote the book on stalwart. "But then, He *is* a nephilim. He is like you in that He is part human, and flawed. This was inevitable. It is obvious we cannot have a human on the Throne."

We moved along. Malach brushed aside low-hanging trees. Most of them cleared my head.

"I'm quite sure you and your father will enjoy leading the humans astray," Malach said.

As far as I knew, this was the longest conversation I'd ever had with God's hitman. "I hate to break this to you, big guy, but I'm not too interested in leading anybody anywhere," I told him.

"You will be in time."

I almost threw my bag of Skittles at him. "I love how everyone has me figured out, like I'm this big, bad time bomb of evil waiting to go off. I'm half-human, Malach. That means I have free will, if not a free destiny."

"Funny, I had this conversation with your father."

I looked at him. "You knew my father?"

"We were friends. At least until he Ascended."

I felt a chill. "What was he like?"

Malach looked at me. "He was like you." He moved ahead of me, taking the lead.

I busied myself with pulling on a pair of leather gloves. I hated them, but I'd be damned if I was going to go pawing through the Berger house and leave fingerprints behind. I wanted to ask Malach more questions about my father, but we were coming upon the house.

Malach pulled his big gun. I pulled my big gun. Together we crossed the backyard and made our way to the back door of the house. The French doors were ajar and the house seemed to be empty, but we still took precautions. I pushed the doors open and Malach cased the place. I was pretty impressed with his technique.

Nothing untoward jumped out at us.

We started moving through the house, checking rooms as we went along, careful to scan behind doors, listening for any sounds, but the house really did seem to be empty.

We found Thom Berger in the kitchen. He was laid out on the kitchen nook table thingy with a number of high-end gourmet knives driven into his wrists to hold him down. A long carving knife projected from his shoulder, just above his heart. He was breathing through bubbles of blood, his chest barely rising and falling.

Malach looked on him with dull interest. I guess when you're an angel and have seen thousands of battles, nothing much impresses you.

"Well, I think Billie was upset," I announced. "You want to stay with him while I check the rest of the house?"

He nodded.

I methodically went through the rest of the rooms on the ground floor, then made my way upstairs. I was careful with each room I came upon, but I was pretty certain that Billie had long since departed—she now had a little piece of me inside of her. I'd know if she was around. I checked the bookshelves in the Bergers' bedroom, and sure enough, the Book of Shadows I'd seen there a few days ago had disappeared. I wasn't overly surprised by that.

A harsh thump from downstairs got my attention. Thom Berger made a strangled barking noise. I carefully wended my way back downstairs, my gun ready.

Malach had removed the knives and had dragged Thom Berger off the blood-soaked breakfast nook table. He now lay on the blood-soaked Italian marble floor, Malach's gigantic hands encasing his narrow, bald head, thumbs over his eyes. He was methodically slamming Thom's head against the floor, and each time it crashed down, the man's body shook and he made those groaning, barking noises.

I stopped to watch. "I thought you were going to call an ambulance."

"He knows where the Arcana are."

"That whole Dominion thing, huh?"

*Bang*, Thom Berger's head came down hard like a gavel, and I think the tile under his head cracked a little. Thom Berger gurgled.

*Bang, bang. Bang!*

I thought about intervening, but Malach said, "He is a sinful man. He has had carnal relations with his daughter. He allowed his wife to die at his daughter's hands. He encouraged it. *Most certainly I tell you, everyone who commits sin is the bondservant of sin.*"

I hunkered down next to Malach. I still thought about intervening. "We should let a court of law sentence him, Malach," I said. "He *is* human. This isn't your jurisdiction."

Malach turned his head and glared at me. "Do not interfere, Nick. The man will tell me where the Arcana are."

"The man can't talk, Malach."

*Bang!* "He does not need to talk. He needs only to *think*." Malach slammed Thom Berger's head down one last time and Thom gasped and stared up at him with dark, pain-filled eyes. Malach took my hand and placed it over Thom's eyes. He placed his hand over mine. The moment he did that, I was struck with a collage of raw, red-rimmed images set in fast forward. I saw the young Billie Berger reading from the old grimoire I'd seen upstairs...Thom Berger having sex with his young daughter...Thom and Carrie Berger arguing, Carrie threatening to leave him forever and take Billie with her...Billie running away, not her choice but her father's who feared his wife would reveal their secret...Billie Berger on the streets of Philadelphia...Carrie Berger in ICU...Thom marrying his new "wife" Rebecca...Billie capturing the angels, consuming their radiant flesh...

I jerked then and fell back onto the floor on my ass, my head swimming in a sickening mental miasma. It had been enough. Too much.

I'd seen. I'd learned. And I'd discovered how wrong I'd been about Billie.

She hadn't returned to Blackwater because she was hopelessly infatuated with her abusive father. She'd returned home because

Thom Berger was the last of the Berger line and Billie needed to breed. She'd needed a child of witchblood, a child of the Berger bloodline. A Wodehouse would have been better, but they were gone except for me, and I couldn't breed. The witch-child was the only way she would ever Ascend...

And that child...

Thom began to scream. He screamed like a machine. He finally understood how he had been used. And now he knew the fate of his child. In his last moments, he had tried to stop Billie. He had tried to be a good father, to do the right thing...

As I watched, blood began seeping from his eyes and mouth and nostrils. It ran in rivulets over his face, down his neck, and into the cracks of the Italian marble floor. There was a brief flash of white light, and both Malach and I lunged back in deference to the being standing there in the middle of the Berger kitchen floor.

My dad had eschewed his usual flamboyant suits for more traditional robes, robes that were iridescent white and gold. He wore a red sash about his waist, and on that sash was his name written in angelic glyphs. His many wings fluttered as he hefted his staff high into the air before using it to spear Thom Berger through the belly. He grinned at me hungrily with great hook-like teeth, and I saw Thom Berger's soul writhe like a worm upon his staff before the two of them disappeared in a flash of searing blue light.

The life went out of Thom Berger's eyes, but his mouth hung open in an eternal scream. Another foot soldier for my dad's army of the dead and the damned.

\* \* \*

Malach, sitting on the floor beside me, told me what he'd seen in the moments before Thom's death. "He said Billie came home and was covered in blood. He tried to stop her before she hurt their child. They fought, and Billie won. She then went to their secret place. It is there that she will consume the witch-child. It is there that she will Ascend."

I stood up slowly, staggering under the weight of the images in my head. There was a part of me that wanted to cry. Finally, I knew why I had hated Thom right from the start. He was so weak. He had found his strength only in the end. Unfortunately, it hadn't saved his soul.

"Malach, we need to find the child. Now." I looked at him. "She's alive and we need to find her before Billie…" I simply could not finish. Maybe my dad was right; maybe I wasn't prepared for this. Maybe I never would be.

Malach climbed to his feet with a great deal more grace than I had. "We must go to their secret place."

I blinked, rubbed at my eyes, still reeling in the aftermath of it all. "What's that supposed to mean?"

"You tell me."

"How should I know?" I yelled, and Malach noticeably flinched. My dad had seriously unnerved him. Not that I could really blame him.

"You are a man of law, Nick…whatever else you might be. Find out." Malach turned away, creaking in his bloodied black leather. "I will wait outside."

"Oh, well, that's just fucking great!" I yelled after him.

Malach slammed the door.

\* \* \*

I started going over the whole house. I had no idea what I was looking for. All I knew for certain was that I had a cooling body lying on the kitchen floor, leaking blood all over the place, and the possibility of the press or the police dropping by anytime. Getting caught in a house with a dead body? Bad. And if Shelley caught me, I might as well be dead. This was pretty much exactly what I needed to solidify my reputation in my community as not only the local nutcase psychic but a psychopathic murderer. On top of it, I couldn't go to the police with any of this. The police would want to investigate. They would want to interrogate me, probably for hours. I didn't have the time for that. *Cassie* didn't have the time.

Since I was wearing gloves, and was pressed for time, I couldn't afford to be delicate. I started in the kitchen, pulling open drawers and dumping their contents onto the floor. I went over counters and into cupboards. Finding nothing that even remotely spoke of secret places, I moved into the living room and started tearing it to pieces, pulling open drawers, scattering the contents of the vast entertainment center, then the end tables and bookshelves. I decided it would help if I knew what the hell I was looking for.

Secret places...I pushed my cop brain into analysis overload. A secret place that Thom and Billie Berger had...a place they went to, most likely to have carnal relations away from the prying eyes of Carrie Berger. That place couldn't be anywhere near here. That was chancing too much.

I stopped when I reached one of those Queen Anne-style rolltop desks set in the corner. It was covered in old family pictures, many dating back to the wartime years. There were pictures of the Bergers in the armed service, pictures of Bergers getting married and baptizing their children. There were pictures of Bergers hunting and fishing. No pictures of Billie or Rebecca. That was smart. I picked up a picture of a young Thom Berger and what might have been his father standing beside the carcass of a newly shot buck. Thom was standing proud, holding his rifle, while his dad was on one knee, holding up the dead deer's head so the full rack of antlers was in the shot. It was a nice picture, the kind of picture I wish I could have taken with my own dad, but it was the background that interested me more. They were standing in front of a cabin tucked away in the deep woods.

I looked for more pictures of the cabin. There were a few, mostly of Thom and his dad. There was one of Thom and Carrie Berger, holding a young baby in their arms. Thom had kept the cabin, but where the hell was it? There were tens of thousands of miles of woodland in the greater Commonwealth of Pennsylvania. The cabin could be anywhere. There were no obvious landmarks, no creeks, only one that showed a valley in the far background. Down in the valley sat a number of almost unidentifiable white blobs. I picked up the picture and held it close to my nose.

The white blobs were symmetrical. Beehives.

I took the picture and stalked outside. Malach was waiting on the back porch, his gun in his hand as if he would shoot anyone who approached the house. The minute he saw me come through the French doors, he turned and eyed me carefully. I could tell the interlude with my dad had shaken him up. I didn't think anything could.

"Did you find the secret place?"

"No," I managed, "but I know how I can." I checked the reception on my phone and then went online. There were three major apiaries in the area, but only one within reasonable driving distance of Blackwater: Sunflower Mountain Apiary Farms. It was ten and a half miles north of here, near Lake Harmony. "Son of a bitch," I said as I planned the quickest route on my phone. I stepped down off the back porch and headed back toward my car, Malach close on my heels.

"What is it?" he asked. I noticed he kept his gun close at hand.

"Shit, I never would have believed it," I said in wonder. "Brownie's wives were right about following the bees."

| 19 |

ON THE DRIVE up to Lake Harmony one of those weird, uncomfortable silences settled in between us. "You know, if I help you," I said, "you really should give me something in return."

Malach smirked in an ugly way. "You are so much like your father, Nick. Always a deal."

"Well, my old man is a bastard, but he's a smart bastard."

Malach busied himself with checking the munitions of his giant gold gun, which was pretty funny when I thought about it. Malach has a magical TV cop gun—it never runs out of bullets. "What do you want, Nick?"

"I want Vivian and Josh safe. I want them off the hit list."

Malach seemed to consider that, then nodded. "I expected you would request that your own name be taken off the list."

"My name will never come off the list," I said. "But Vivian and Josh have done nothing wrong. They've broken none of your laws. Josh isn't even a daemon. You guys have no right hunting them."

"But the woman is a daemon."

"A daemon who has done nothing wrong."

"Except to kill two men."

"One was hurting her. The other was an accident."

Malach snorted. "The daemon is a dangerous, untrained force, Nick."

"Then I'll train her. I'll teach her to control herself and her power." I glared over at him. I can glare too. "This is non-negotiable, Malach. You guys back off Vivian and Josh or I'll dump your sorry angelic ass on the side of this road and go back home and let you deal with the Arcana on your own. I have things to do, you know."

That wasn't exactly true. I knew that Cassie Berger was at the cabin, and I meant to find her, but Malach didn't have to know how deeply I was invested in this. Hopefully, he couldn't read my mind. If he could, my bluff was pretty damned useless. I knew angels could read each other's minds, a sort of gigantic hive consciousness. It was the reason why the death of one angel attracted more angels. Barring some kind of ward, every angel could listen to the thoughts and emotions of every other angel. And I had just learned that angels could also read the minds of humans—which, I admit, had made me kind of jealous. Still, I didn't know if the same was true of demon or daemon minds. Demons are, by their very nature (and often their own decision) cut off from the Throne. Did that mean they were cut off from the groupthink as well?

Malach nodded. "Very well. Their names will be taken off the list." That made me breathe a giant mental sigh of relief. "But the Seraphs and Cherubim will continue to hunt you, you realize."

"And in other news, the sky was blue today and water was wet."

As usual, Malach just stared at me. I wished he would get a sense of humor already.

About ten minutes later, we reached the outskirts of Lake Harmony. I followed Google Maps around the lake to the apiary, which was located in a deep valley about five miles wide. In this part of Pennsylvania, with the ground being so rocky, about the only things that grew in abundance were grapes and beehives. I followed the map to the edge of the lake, and soon we started seeing clusters of summer cabins and lake houses around the edges of Lake Harmony.

I kept driving until they started thinning out. The cabin in the picture had looked pretty isolated.

I pulled into the little parking lot of a Uni-Mart that likely served the whole community.

Malach said, "What are you doing?"

"Don't get your panties in a twist. I'll be right back."

Inside the shop, I got directions to the Berger cabin by telling them I was Rebecca Berger's cousin and I meant to surprise her. Hey, it wasn't entirely a lie. I bought a pack of Camels and some candy corn to cover my tracks. I even bought Malach a packet of root beer float candies. I don't know why, but he just seemed like a root beer float candy kind of guy.

Malach analyzed the candy as if it was a species of off-world life as I drove up a long, twisty road surrounded on both sides by heavy fall brush that scraped the sides of the Monaco. "This is full of toxins," he finally declared.

"That's why they're fun."

"We should stop now," he said. "The Arcana may detect us."

I dragged on my Camel and let the smoke percolate out my nose and into the closed-up car. Malach coughed. "The Arcana already detect us. Billie drank my blood and ate a good chunk out of my arm, Malach. Do you honestly think she doesn't know we're coming?"

Up ahead I spotted a cabin, and a Jeep parked on the side of the road. It wasn't the Bergers' SUV, but I bet it belonged to Billie Berger nonetheless. I got out and Malach got out with me. I checked my gun. Malach checked his.

I glanced up at the sky. It was overcast, but the fresh orange sun was slowly burning through the early morning mist. It wasn't yet high noon, but we were about to have a showdown.

\* \* \*

The Berger cabin rested on an overlook. Behind it was the deep, autumn-brown valley full of apiary beehives that I'd seen in the photograph. I thought how well this place must have served Thom and Billie Berger's needs throughout the years. It was high enough to see someone coming, but isolated enough that if they were headed your way, you knew they had business with you. Since the apiary was almost in their backyard, the other denizens of Harmony Lake probably avoided this place like the plague. There's nothing like ornery nesting honeybees getting into your car.

Malach and I stalked down the rough gravel driveway to the cabin. We walked side by side, skirmish-style. I felt strangely like an Old West gunfighter on my way to a gunfight. Malach looked like one in his long black duster. The cabin looked unnervingly empty and composed, all its pieces in place like a postcard.

Malach said, "There's someone inside."

"Can you tell who?"

"No. But human."

Not Billie, then. I would sense her. She was carrying a little piece of me inside her.

We reached the front door and moved to either side. Since I was on the side with the doorknob, I reached for it and turned it, trying to make as little noise as possible. "Locked."

"Shoot it."

I did. The rapport echoed through the valley below.

Malach turned and elbowed the door in. He barely seemed to break a sweat, and the whole door went down in pieces. It just wasn't fair that someone should be able to do that, even an angel. At the same time, he managed to move to my side with remarkable grace and case the inside of the cabin.

"Anything?"

"No." He moved inside.

I followed, sort of using Malach as a shield. I mean, I liked him as my partner, but if he wanted to take one for the home team, who was I to complain? We were operating like SWAT, I realized, which was weird when you thought about it. I felt like I was living a primetime TV cop show—*The Angel and the Daemon*, coming to CBS this fall! Without saying a word, we split up and started going over the whole cabin. It was a two-story luxury chalet, and the upper floor was a loft area.

I took the upstairs like last time. I discovered a loft with a bureau, writing desk, and sofa bed. Though tidy, the closed-up space smelled damp and acidic, like urine. Stains from human waste and blood scarred the floor. A package of animal crackers lay scattered across the throw rug. Most had been eaten. This must be Cassie's room, I thought. I felt the vomit rise slowly in my throat. I just knew I had come too late.

Then I heard muffled crying noises coming from beneath the sofa bed pushed into one corner. The crying was breathy and feral, like a cat trapped in a tight spot. When I was halfway across the room, I got down on my hands and knees, the Tanaka close at hand, and peered under the bed. Enough dirty morning light slanted through the smeary loft window to make out a small, huddled human package under the bed. The smell it gave off, a mixture of old, sick vomit and human waste, made me want to heave. The sight of it made me want to cry.

It was Cassie Berger.

"Well, hello there, honeybee," I said.

The filthy little baby rubbed at her face and wet nose, then put her fingers in her mouth. She peered at me with huge, white, lemur eyes and made a snuffling noise like a nervous animal.

"Oh, honeybee, I need you to come out of there," I said, wondering if I'd have any better luck with Cassie Berger than I had with Tiger. "You can't stay here, baby girl. I need to take you home."

Cassie snuffled and stayed put, but my adventures with Tiger had at least given me an idea. I just didn't have the heart to force her out from under the bed, not after what she'd likely been through, so I reached into my jacket pocket and offered her some of the candy corn.

"Come on, honeybee. I have some food for you."

I knew Cassie was afraid—I couldn't blame her in the least—but hunger made her brave. Hunger drew her out. If I had been surviving for four days on nothing but a small package of animal crackers I would have gone to anyone, too, even my father. I sat down on the floor and held very still as she crawled awkwardly out from under the bed. Her little limbs were covered in bite marks. Some were days old and leaky and infected, others new. They were big bites, strategically placed to keep the little witch-girl alive while Billie fed off her blood and meat and power without killing her.

I waited. The Tay-Sachs didn't make it any easier for her, but little Cassie stared at me with determination. She crawled across the floor and climbed into my lap and started eating the candy corn right out of my hands. I'd never had much experience with children. Mostly, like pets, they avoided me like the plague. But as Cassie Berger nibbled the candy corn excitedly out of my hand and then begged for more, I held her close and came to a strange realization.

I loved Cassie. I hated my father because he was always right. And I hoped that Billie Berger had run far, far away. Because when I found her, I was going to put a fucking bullet in her skull.

\* \* \*

I settled Cassie Berger on the bed. I wrapped my coat around her and gave her my bag of candy corn to eat. I was about to call down to Malach when the window behind me shattered inward like someone had punched a giant fist through it. Glass raked across my back, but luckily, my body shielded Cassie. I turned and pulled my gun at the same time. I fired on the almost Medusan visage of Billie Berger crawling through the broken shards of the window. Her visage was nearly blinding, but through the glow of her stolen power, I recognized six wings beating at the air. Billie Berger was still Ascending. Soon she would have eight wings, the mark of an archangel.

My first shot nailed her in the head, the .50 round atomizing it. When the debris cleared, I saw a headless Billie Berger still crawling through the window, through the glass and the shattered window frame. I thought it was some delayed death thing but the body just kept on coming. A part of me wanted to deny this thing. My hands told my brain they weren't interested in doing anything except stopping the monster coming after me and took aim again, but Billie moved too fast. She crawled across the floor with insane grace, sans head. Then she was upon me.

She was incredibly strong. She grabbed my gun hand and slammed it down onto the floor. The gun went flying into a corner. She held me down with her other hand. Her back arched like a woman in the throes of climax, and then her spine seemed to extend, a weird, bony knob forming at the tip. The knob grew in size, assuming a smooth, skull-like shape in mere seconds. Blood, muscle, and gristle crawled across the bone like some kind of weird, time-lapse photography film, then liquid skin flowed over it all and a face formed. Dark blonde hair burst like a net around Billie's savage, black-eyed face, and then she was whole once more.

Billie tried to bite me again with her newfound teeth.

I gripped her hair—it felt wet and alive, her entire head covered in a newborn mucus—and held it back, pulling her face away from me. Her wings flickered in irritation. If *this* was what happened when she bit me once, I did not want a repeat performance. Another bite and I knew she would take the rest of my power. She would Ascend. Then we all would suffer.

Billie growled, her jaws snapping reflexively like some rabid wild animal. Her wings beat at me, nearly blinding me in their radiance. I heard footsteps on the stairs, faster than anything human. "Shoot her, Malach!" I screamed, straining with all my strength to keep her teeth away from me. "Shoot her now!"

Before that could happen, Billie let go and rolled off me. Malach came bursting through the door, his gun drawn. I expected Billie to duck to one side, as any sane person would, but then I realized my mistake. Billie wasn't human anymore. She wasn't *anything* anymore. Instead of avoiding the shot, she took it full in the chest. Malach's gun left an absolutely ginormous hole. I swear a small child could have crawled through it—not that Billie was going to allow something like that to ruin her day. She charged Malach, an athame in her upraised hand, a gunshot wound burned through the middle part of her body. Malach had forgotten that Billie was now more than human.

With a wet, warbling scream, Billie was upon him. She plunged the athame into the side of Malach's neck. Malach screamed and blue blood burst heavenward. I had never heard Malach scream before. I had never heard anything scream like Malach screamed. It was the kind of sound that every cell in the body responds to. For a moment, I was absolutely paralyzed by the sound of it, and by the sight of Malach writhing in agony through the hole in Billie's body. Then, seconds later, the rift in her body seamlessly sealed itself up.

Malach went down hard, like someone had exploded a grenade in his face, Billie on top of him.

Billie bent her head and bit into the side of Malach's neck. Malach roared as Billie began to feed.

I stood up and aimed the Tanaka at Cassie. I said, "Billie, turn around! Turn around or I'll shoot your daughter!"

Billie stopped feeding on Malach and turned to face me. Her face and breasts were soaked in Malach's pale blue gore. Her eyes shone blindly, like portals into an unknowable white hell. I wondered if I was seeing God's eyes.

"Lord of Flies," she said.

"Yeah, that's me," I answered. It broke my heart to have to aim a gun at Cassie Berger's head as the little girl cowered there on the bed, but I didn't know how else to get Billie's attention. "Let Malach go or I'll kill the witch-child. No more power for you."

Billie straightened up and regarded me carefully. She was almost painful to look upon, not as painful as my dad when in archangel mode, but close. It was like staring into the sun. "You are the Evil One," she said. "The new young Lucifer. I *know* you. You should die."

I narrowed my eyes at her but forced my hand not to waver where I pointed the gun at Cassie's head. "You can call me all the names you want, bitch, but at least I don't go around eating my own children."

She bared her teeth, strong and white and faintly hooked. They were hungry angel teeth. "You will eat the world, Dragon." She smiled, wisely, the way my dad can. "You will walk the earth, and where you walk, hell will follow you. You will bring hell to this earth, devil, you and your Whore of Babylon." She extended her hand and made the sign of the ward, two fingers out and two down. "Satan," she shouted, "Get. Thee. Down!"

I braced myself and waited for a tremendous otherworldly power to force me to my knees, but nothing happened. I wondered about that. And then it hit me. I knew. I knew and I laughed. Emily had power over me because she *believed*. It was her faith that gave her power. "You don't believe, Billie," I said, dropping the gun. It was useless to me now. "Who does God pray to, after all?" I pulled the angel athame out of my boot and approached her.

Billie looked at me in rage, and then in fear. All her badassery seemed to vanish in that moment. "The Throne is empty, devil," she told me, stumbling back away from me. "Would you keep it that way?"

I smiled. I knew it was an evil smile. I even enjoyed it. "I'd rather have an empty Throne than a God that eats angels and children."

I saw real panic in her eyes. She turned to grab at the athame that was still stuck in Malach's shoulder, but it was wedged in his flesh. Anyway, I was faster than she was. I was on her in seconds. I grabbed a greasy handful of her hair. I rocked her back against the front of my body until her back was bowed and her belly fully exposed. I plunged the angel athame into it. The blade had been baptized in the blood of her victims, the metal pure white like bone, and sharper than a tooth. Billie screamed. Her wings shushed all around me. Her arms flailed, hands grasping at air as if to beseech someone. But *she* was God…or the closest thing to it at the moment. There was no one else for her to cry to. I kept my hand firmly entrenched in her hair and my athame buried in her belly. I dragged the athame up, unzipping her flesh easily. Then I dropped the knife and I sank my hand up to the forearm in her burning wet guts until I found what I was looking for.

It burned cold. Somehow, I just wasn't surprised. I closed my hand over Billie's second heart and ripped it from her belly. Some of her gory insides came out with it like a net, a deep, troubling merlot color. She had not yet made the full transformation to a blue-blooded angel, but she was close. Billie fell limp in my arms, the light slowly fading from her eyes. In the last seconds, I showed her what I held. It burned bright white in my hand, like a dove on fire, but the moment I clenched my fist, the light began to fade and the heart began to harden. In mere seconds, I held only dry powdery white angel ash in my hand. I let it crumble between my fingers.

"Devil," she said with her rattling last breath.

"Say hello to my dad when you see him," I told her. I let her go and she crumpled lifelessly to the floor at my feet.

In the silence that followed, Cassie began to cry.

## | 20 |

I SPENT TEN hours in interrogation down at the Blackwater Police Department. They tried to book me on manslaughter—I had been found with Billie's blood all over me—but I told them the truth. Billie had come after me when she'd realized I'd found her daughter and planned to take her away. She was insane, her strength enormous. She'd gotten the gun out of my hand, so I had been forced to use the only weapon I had available to me, the athame I used in ritual Wiccan practice.

In general, I've found that the truth usually works out pretty well; you just have to remember to remove the supernatural parts. When they questioned me on how I knew about the cabin, I again told them the truth: I saw photographs in the house when I'd been there. I had just followed my nose, with a little help from Google and the kind folks down at the Uni-Mart who had told me the location of Thom Berger's cabin.

There was nothing to link me to the murder of Thom Berger—Billie took the heat for that one. Actually, she took the heat for everything. A forensic doctor was able to match Billie's bite to the marks on little Cassie's arms and legs, so the idea that Billie had been insane, killed her husband, and was trying to feed on her own daughter wasn't entirely farfetched. Weird and sad, and great fodder for Shelley Preston and Mountaintop Radio, but not impossible.

I suggested DNA testing to prove what I already knew to be true, that Rebecca Berger and Billie Berger were the same person, but by then, the forensic team was already on my side. After all, Tay-Sachs Syndrome is most commonly caused by close inbreeding—or so they told me.

Two days later, the case mounted against dead Billie Berger disqualified the evidence found on Vivian's computer, which led to Vivian's charges being dropped. Microscopic traces of Brittany's blood had been found on a hammer in the Berger cabin. The police believed that Billie Berger had gone to Vivian's house to plant evidence on her computer, but Brittany had surprised her when she'd come home early after breaking up with her cheating boyfriend Mark. Since Billie couldn't allow Brittany to talk, she had taken a hammer to the girl, then gotten the body into the trunk of Brittany's car and driven her to a secluded area. I actually believed Billie's choice of victim had been more personal and premeditated, but I kept my mouth shut on that one. I figured if it ain't broke, don't fix it.

I think Sheriff Ben felt I knew more than I was letting on, but he was bound by the law, and the law requires evidence. I knew he'd keep the kachina doll, just like I knew he'd be keeping an eye on me from now on. I'm pretty sure he couldn't decide if I was a hero or a villain. Funny, neither could I. Still, he couldn't hold me on suspicion of murder without evidence.

For little Cassie Berger, it was touch and go for a while, but the hospital filled her full of food and antibiotics, and bound all her terrible bite marks with bandages. It turned out she was a much tougher young lady than she seemed.

When I heard that she was asking for candy—candy corn, to be specific—I went to see her at the hospital. I brought candy corn and candy pumpkins and sugar Peeps. The nurses let me sit with her in bed and feed Cassie candy while they looked on in horror. I even brought a book with me, *The Velveteen Rabbit*, which was probably my favorite book growing up. Cassie loved it. She fell asleep before the Velveteen Rabbit became a real rabbit, but I knew I'd be back the following day to finish the book with her.

I left the book with Cassie and went downstairs to visit the gift shop. I hunted high and low until I found a rabbit that looked very much like the Velveteen Rabbit, though plush. I thought maybe I'd tell Cassie it was magic the next time I saw her, that the rabbit in the story had become a real toy rabbit. The idea excited me. My dad never read me any books when I was growing up. He never told me about magic. I had had to learn everything on my own.

While I was shopping, I noticed someone very familiar hanging out in the waiting room. The shop had a little section of old, used books and VHS tapes, so I went over them until I found the perfect gift, then took my purchases to the counter.

Malach was leaning against the wall, watching the nervous people in the waiting room with cool, remote eyes, when I stepped out of the gift shop. "You saw the girl," he said at once.

"You're not hunting her, are you?" I said. I decided that if Malach was contemplating hurting little Cassie, I might have to bust him up. How I would do that I didn't know, but I'd find a way.

"There is something wrong with her."

I nodded at that. "Billie bore Cassie after she'd begun the ritual of eating angel flesh. So Cassie is part angel as well as part witch, which was the reason Billie was eating her child slowly, a bite at a time. That about cover it?"

"Something like that."

"That makes her a nephilim, not a daemon, Malach."

"Yes. I know."

As far as I was aware, nephilim, though not exactly encouraged, were not really hunted either, not like we daemons are. After all, we daemons are *evil*...or so I've been given to understand. I turned to glare at Malach. I can glare as fiercely as any angel. "You don't honestly believe that I would hurt Cassie?"

Malach considered that. "No."

It occurred to me that despite being an angel of death, Malach wasn't the kind of dude to just hang around hospitals, waiting for people to die. He was more the type to put people in the hospital. I didn't think he was there just to see me. Malach doesn't like me that much. He must be there for Cassie, I thought. Who knows? Maybe he considered her a viable candidate for the Throne—a thought that made me smile. If that was true, Cassie Berger had the best guardian angel *ever*. "I'll keep an eye on her too," I said, and winked.

Malach didn't say anything, and his expression did not change, but we shared a moment of complete understanding. He stared down at his feet. "Thank you," he said as stiffly and cordially as anyone I've ever seen. I could tell it took a lot of pride out of him to say those words.

"It bothers you that the Throne's empty, doesn't it?" I said.

Malach shrugged his big linebacker shoulder. "We're entering bad times, Nick. Everything's changing. Everything's...*wrong*."

"Tell me about it. Any particular reason for your change of heart regarding me?"

"I prefer the devil I know."

Now that did make me smile. Not that he'd called me a devil, but that he trusted me at least enough to not shoot me today. That's saying a lot, where Malach is concerned. I reached into my gift bag and retrieved the worn VHS copy of *Terminator 2* and handed it to him. I hoped he had a VCR, wherever he lived. Or maybe Malach just used osmosis to watch movies? It wouldn't surprise me. "Just remember your promise, big guy. Hasta la vista," I told him and started for the hospital exit.

\* \* \*

I kept my promise. On the day the police released Vivian, I drove her, Josh, and Tiger down to Indian Mountain Lake Park. I spread a blanket on the soft, springy grass by the waterside and set out some coffees I had bought from Dunkin Donuts. Josh took his coffee and let Tiger pilot him along the edge of the lake. Tiger trotted excitedly through the long fall grass, checking out the late season wildflowers and the catfish that wriggled along the edges of the shore.

Meanwhile, I set out a box of glazed chocolate and jelly-filled donuts. "I didn't know what kind you liked," I confessed to Vivian. "I forgot to ask. I'm sorry."

Vivian knelt down beside me on the blanket. She looked stunning in her skin-tight blue jeans and red halter top knotted under her breasts. She wore an adorable belly ring, a diamond stud with a little dangling pendant in the form of Maleficent from *Sleeping Beauty*. When I asked her about it, she told me Maleficent was her favorite Disney character of all time, and she wished she had gone off with the prince instead of Princess Aurora because she was much sexier, in her opinion.

I laughed at that.

She turned to me, hooked her arms around my neck, and pulled me down for a kiss. It was a powerfully hungry kiss. I thought about that expression, *Absence makes the heart grow fonder*, and wondered what would have happened had we been parted for more than a few days. Vivian would likely have thrown me to the ground and had her way with me—not that I would have necessarily protested that. As it was, she pushed me down onto the blanket and climbed on top of me. I tried to move, to slide my hands around her beautiful warm curves, but she held me down and kissed my mouth and inside my mouth. As always, I was both pleased and surprised by her aggression.

When she finally let me breathe again, I said, "I'll bring donuts more often."

"Silly man."

We made out for a few more minutes like a couple of randy teenagers until Vivian's hands began to wander toward the danger zone. It felt good, Vivian on top of me and the warm Indian summer beating down on us both. I loved how she took charge, how she called the shots in our lovemaking, but as her hand went for my cock I said, "You know, your brother could wander back at any time."

Disappointed, she slid to one side of me on the blanket and propped herself up on an elbow. For someone who had just made me a very happy man, she looked troubled.

"Is something wrong?" I asked.

"I keep thinking about Billie. About how this is basically my fault."

"How is any of this basically your fault?"

She frowned. "I mean...I knew Billie. And Billie knew all my secrets growing up. She knew about Mr. McCarty and the janitor. I can't help but feel that's where all this began...with her looking for a way to hurt her dad."

"The Bergers had been into magic a long, long time, Vivian. I saw the book that Billie used to read. It was centuries old. She left home specifically to find the Arcana that she'd read about in those pages. That's extremely premeditated and not at all your fault."

"But she might not have pursued it if she didn't know what I could do."

I looked at her earnestly. "Billie made her own decisions, Viv. That has nothing to do with you. You have your own path. And your own set of challenges ahead of you."

She thought about that some before smiling at me. "So you want to come by my place tonight and help me pack? We could have some fun afterward." Her smile was very sexy and very evil.

I had found Vivian a better apartment, one in a renovated, deconsecrated church. It was still holy ground...just not ground that could hurt someone like her, or me. I was fairly certain Malach would keep his promise, but I wasn't sure about the other angels, especially the ones under Gabe's new regime. I knew there was going to be trouble. A lot of it. Until I'd taught her at least the rudiments of magic, I wanted Vivian safe. Unfortunately, by helping Vivian find the apartment, I had inadvertently volunteered myself to help her move into it as well.

I reached for her. I cupped her cheek in my hand and ran my thumb across her wet lips. "I'll come by after I close the shop," I said. "But it'll be late."

Her smile never slipped. "Then I guess we'll just have to concentrate on having fun tonight. Do you have handcuffs?"

"*Handcuffs?* Well, I *was* a cop."

"Good."

"But they hurt," I warned her.

Vivian smiled slyly. "I didn't say they were for *me*."

"You're bad," I laughed, a little nervously. "I'm really not into that, you know."

"So prudish."

"You expect me to be a deviant sexual maniac?"

Vivian shrugged, tossing her hair over a shoulder. "You're the Devil's son, Nick. I don't know what to expect."

"I'm just a regular guy."

"A regular guy who just happens to be a witch, a daemon, and a former cop."

"That too." I watched her. I watched some orangey fall maple leaves drift down and catch in her hair. A honeybee drifted by. I was seeing an awful lot of bees lately, which was unusual this late in the season. It made me wonder if they weren't Vivian's animal familiar, which would be awfully cool—and a great deal less trouble than fauns. "It really doesn't bother you, all this weird stuff?" I asked with genuine interest.

Vivian shrugged. "I think it's fun."

"Fun."

"How many girls can say they're the Devil's concubine and be perfectly honest about it?"

I picked up her wrist and looked at the scars that still looked so raw and painful. Vivian said they didn't hurt at all. I thought she was amazing. "Do you regret it yet?"

"No. Why should I regret it? I said I wanted to belong to you. I still do."

"You might think differently when I have to...take over the family business."

"You mean go to hell."

"You're not even afraid of that?"

"Why should I be afraid?" She reached out and ran her fingers over my face. "You'll be the man in charge. The head honcho of the demon world."

"Don't remind me."

"Why does it bother you?" she asked, pulling me close against her. That made me happy again. "You'll get to torment people like Billie Berger for millennia. I can think of worse jobs. I'm working one of them right now at the steakhouse."

I shook my head in amazement. "Maybe I should put you in charge."

Vivian laughed and kissed me breathless again, but in the moments before she did, I caught a hungry gleam in her eyes. Her hands started wandering again. The things I had told her had turned her on. I started wondering if something like that was good or bad, but then I just gave in to kissing her like any regular guy would.

Nick Englebrecht Will Return in<br>
**The Devil Dances**

# ABOUT THE AUTHOR

**K.H. Koehler** is the author of various novels and novellas in the genres of horror, SF, dark fantasy, steampunk, and young and new adult. She is the owner of KH Koehler Books and KH Koehler Design, which specializes in graphic design and professional copyediting. Her books are widely available at all major online distributors and her covers have appeared on numerous books in many different genres. Her short work has appeared in various anthologies, and her novel series include *The Kaiju Hunter*, *A Clockwork Vampire*, *The Nick Englebrecht Mysteries*, and *The Archeologists*. She is the author of multiple Amazon bestsellers and was one of the founders and chief editors of KHP Publishers, which published genre fiction from 2001 to 2015. She has over fifteen years of experience in the publishing industry as a writer, ghostwriter, copyeditor, commercial book cover designer, formatter, and marketer. Visit her website at https://khkoehler.net.

www.ingramcontent.com/pod-product-compliance
Lightning Source LLC
LaVergne TN
LVHW030321070526
838199LV00069B/6520